Praise for Lutz Bassmann

"Ambiguity and gloom blend in this collection of stories to work the reader into a wonderful confusion." —*Full Stop*

"No one has to be schooled in the arcana of post-exoticism to see that We Monks and Soldiers is a gorgeously patterned and deeply moving work." —*The Collagist*

"A continually changing, continually new poetic force."
—**Christophe Kantcheff,** *Politis*

"Between a fragile lyricism and an almost silent poetic expression of an absolute, inevitable devastation." —**Hugo Pradelle,** *La Quinzaine Littéraire*

"Vividly imagined, thought provoking and spare, this is an unusual collection . . . worth searching out." —**Sandy Amazeen,** *Monsters and Critics*

**Also by
Lutz Bassmann**

We Monks and Soldiers

BLACK VILLAGE

LUTZ BASSMANN

Translated from the French by
Jeffrey Zuckerman

OPEN LETTER
LITERARY TRANSLATIONS FROM THE UNIVERSITY OF ROCHESTER

Originally published as *Black Village* © Éditions Verdier, 2017
Translation copyright © 2022 by Jeffrey Zuckerman

First edition, 2022

Library of Congress Cataloging-in-Publication Data: Available.
ISBN-13: 978-1-948830-43-0 / ISBN-10: 1-948830-43-4

*This work received support from the French Ministry of Foreign Affairs and the Cultural
Services of the French Embassy in the United States through their publishing assistance program.*

*This project is supported in part by an award from the National Endowment for the Arts
and the New York State Council on the Arts with the support of Governor
Andrew M. Cuomo and the New York State Legislature.*

Printed on acid-free paper in the United States of America.

Cover Design by Anne Jordan
Interior Design by Anthony Blake

Open Letter is the University of Rochester's nonprofit, literary translation press:
Dewey Hall 1-219, Box 278968, Rochester, NY 14627

www.openletterbooks.org

BLACK VILLAGE

Introduction

I READ *BLACK VILLAGE* WHILE OVERLANDING beside a clear creek
in the Bridger Teton national forest. It was me, my wife, and our
young daughter, a dozen miles off the main road and deeper into the
wild of Wyoming than I was comfortable with. It should have been
idyllic. Mountains spearing the sky. The gentle bend of the creek, its
cool water singing in a thousand voices over the rocks. The problem
is we aren't "camping people." I don't even own hiking boots. But my
wife thought it would be good for us. Filtering water from a stream.
No lights. No services. Just the three of us. Getting away. Getting
lost. But for me it only highlighted how incapable I was at doing
anything. Everything I thought I knew was a struggle out there. I
wasn't allowed to build a fire because of drought. So we brushed
our teeth in darkness. I fumbled with my socks, put them on wrong
side out. Using the bathroom required a spoon and a prayer that
nothing would eat me while I crouched defenselessly. And I had
to wait an eternity for water to boil on the small stove. Out there
I burned through my flashlight batteries reading Lutz Bassmann's
Black Village late into the night. Like Bassmann's characters, I felt
utterly fallible. Helpless. Incapable of doing anything right. But it
was okay. The point was just being there, and we were. Surviving in
the mountains. I got that part right.

Our first morning we hiked to a craggy trailhead that forked into three paths. My wife suggested we take the eight-mile waterfall trail. My daughter said she wanted the path with least amount of bees. I used my pinky to measure if it was eight miles there and back, or just eight miles there. But murder bees or getting stranded in the woods quickly became the least of my worries. Stapled next to the trail map was a sign to remind hikers that everything out here would kill us. It had a clipart picture of a bear head on it. Teeth out, head tilted to the side. This was grizzly territory. And in a few neat bullet points the sign listed all the skills I'd need to defend myself from an apex predator. I was to stand my ground—never run. Stand tall and be loud. And if the bear decided it still wanted to eat me, play dead. But while playing dead, if the bear still tried to eat me, only then was I to "fight like hell."

The image of me "fighting like hell" to ward of a grizzly. I chuckled as I adjusted the straps on my little backpack. I was going to get killed over a granola bar. I was clueless, ill-prepared. But we had our hiking shorts on. And there was mountain water in our canteens.

The final bullet advised that we carry bear spray. This was communicated in all caps with a few too many exclamation points. It seemed like more than a suggestion. "I don't have any bear spray," I told my wife. She gave me that look that said I was total idiot. I shrugged. "I don't even own a pocketknife." But I told her I could fix it. And I ran back to our camp and grabbed the fire extinguisher from our car.

"What are you going to do with that?" my daughter said.

"I'll spray it," I said. My wife looked on with amusement. "I don't know if you've ever been sprayed with a fire extinguisher . . . it's pretty surprising. I'd definitely run away."

On the trail the fire extinguisher shifted in my backpack. Jabbing one kidney then the next. I wasn't sure if I should be running point or taking up the rear. But I was certain—front or back—my end was nigh. I scanned the trail. Each shadow was a predator. Every bush hid some unknown danger. Out there, hopelessly unprepared, I felt like the soldier fresh out of boot camp. The one who dies first in the movie when it's time for patrol.

Everything was worse at night. In blindness the creek became a roiling cauldron. The hoot of the owls told the whole forest where to find us. In Bassmann's *Black Village* there were "immeasurable fears and darknesses" that made it impossible to keep making it through their perils. And oh, how aware of them I had become. I listened intently for a snapping branch, the low huff of animal breath. Even if I got a warning, I wasn't sure I'd be able to pull the pin fast enough on the fire extinguisher. But I kept it by our flimsy screen door. I couldn't rest, so I by candlelight I slipped back into *Black Village*. I got lost in Bassmann's world of rancor and darkness, a place where the pathetic glow of a match pulses fragilely, where "lamplight was just about to die . . ."

I listened to my family as they slept without a care. I kissed them and watched the spray of stars above us. How clean and cold the night was. Stirring but somehow still. I took in, as described aptly by Bassmann, the "black breath of the universe" before closing my eyes. And that's when I felt it. I was neither alive nor dead. I was something else. Someplace else. In that impossible darkness I understood that nothing out here wanted to kill me. It was far worse. Whether I lived or died, this place was totally indifferent.

—BRIAN WOOD
Gros Ventre Wilderness, Wyoming

1. Black 1

VERY SLOWLY, GOODMANN MADE SOME LIGHT. Deep in his pockets were powder and grease that he had carried for some years now, protecting them from rain and dust, never trading them for food even in the worst moments of his hunger. He had preserved them from ruin, foreseeing this moment when we would no longer be able to bear this darkness, and ever since the outset, many years earlier, he had been talking to us about them. He overstated their properties and wore out superlatives in calling them "luminescent tallows," "wonderfully illuminating greases," "nearly smokeless powders," and so on. We had waited a long time, reassured in our knowledge that this hallowed flame could be found on Goodmann's body. Regularly, at least twice every year, Goodmann waxed poetic to us about the treasures he carried and promised us that he would use them wisely, when all these immeasurable fears and darknesses made it impossible for us to keep making our way through these perils. And now the time had come.

We listened to Goodmann clumsily handling, one by one, these powders that he had kept in often-unsuitable boxes or in salt shakers with covers that time had pummeled and that now barely acceded to his ministrations, resisting and crumbling beneath his fingers. The powders ended up scattered around us, wasted and no longer usable. Goodmann, all our eyes on him, said nothing, did not groan in frustration, but we heard his increasingly halting breaths, we suffered with him in empathy and we felt the horror of this failure on so many levels, which threatened to affect us and strike us and disappoint us and dismay us—him as well as us—in equal measure. The small packets split open as soon as they neared the pads of his fingers or the edges of his fingernails: the dwarf boxes didn't open, they resisted Goodmann's especially careful attempts, then fell on the ground or shattered, burst, freed with a brief sigh and a small irretrievable cloud. Based on the noise, we deduced that we were on a floorboard, on a solid wood pathway, on a well-built footbridge, or a theater stage. Goodmann opened the sachets of luminescent tallows with extreme patience, slowing his movements, hoping to give the tallows some wisdom through this slowness. But nothing doing.

Then a flame, fat as a soybean seed, and hardly brighter, burst on Goodmann's left hand, atop the back of his left hand, close to the fork between his ring and middle fingers.

— Keep your distance, Goodmann ordered.

— Careful, I said. If the fire spreads, your hand will burn.

— The flame has to start with grease, Myriam, our little sister, said. If the flame starts on your hand, your hand will burn.

— Then what? Goodmann asked.

— Add some grease, Myriam said.

— There's no more grease, Goodmann said. The grease is gone. Keep your distance.

An hour went by in stillness. The flame wavered between nothingness and nonexistence, and Goodmann along with us worriedly watched its fragility, with such worry, with such fragility that all three of us remained paralyzed, almost breathless. Although we hadn't seen the least light in years, we were aware that this pathetic gleam could go out any second now, and that nothing else was lit, at least in the sense we generally gave that word. Goodmann's left hand didn't tremble, but it was so scarcely lit that all it took was an unintentional blink for us never to be able to find it again in the depths of the thick darkness our eyes were scrutinizing. With the slightest blink, it disappeared.

— Keep your distance, Goodmann reminded us.

We kept our distance. For several reasons. The first was that we respected each other, and when one of us phrased a suggestion as an order, we followed it without question. The second was that Goodmann, for months now, had taken charge of our team's technical matters, and so had been granted the authority to run our communal existence. The third was that this chance of light had to be preserved at all costs and therefore could not be put at risk by inopportune movements.

A second hour went by, then there was a noise from the flame and from Goodmann: by Goodmann's calcinable bones, by his worn-out flesh, by his whitish tendons, by his hardened, mummified skin, by his fissures, by his old fissures: the flame was catching.

— The flame's catching, Myriam said.

— Yes, Goodmann said. But don't presume this is the end of it.

— Your hand will burn, Myriam said, worried.

— Don't presume this is the end of it, Goodmann repeated.

His intonation was unusual.

— Don't move unless I tell you to, he continued.

Now that the flame had caught, his face could finally be seen. Ours could, as well. We had made our way without light for so long that the mere idea of having a physiognomy rose up in us, a brutal realization so obscene as to petrify us. Myriam bit her lips to keep from shrieking in terror. Goodmann's head was that of a hairy wolf, a tattered head with exceedingly black eyes deep within their sunken sockets, at once watchful and delirious. Myriam no longer looked like the bunkhouse princess we'd remembered, she had a semi-human snout deformed by the crusts of soot that had become embedded over the months; her eyes were buried beneath bushy, unruly brows, they seemed shabbily phosphorescent, shaken by bouts of insanity. As for me, Myriam told me later, I seemed to have been tarred then harrowed by a decrepit tool, a comb perhaps. Our bodies had hardly fared any better.

— I see your faces, I said.

— Shut it, Tassili, Goodmann said. Don't presume this is the end of it.

— Maybe that's what the light is for, I said.

— For what? Myriam asked.

— The end, I said.

— Not at all, Goodmann said. If it's for anything, it's only for the beginning.

Goodmann was grimacing in pain, because the flame was trying to feed on the fingers of his left hand, which he was now holding up like a torch.

— You're in danger of getting eaten up, Myriam declared.

— It's slow fire, Goodmann said, very slow fire. There's enough for days and even years. Enough light for all three of us until the end. I mean until we're out of here.

Here.

Now the surroundings were clearer. We were inside a trench built wholly of wooden logs, from firs I think, suitably stripped of their branches and set tightly, except for an arrow slit I was standing close to, but which overlooked nothing more than a black land-scape, maybe just earth, or some black tunnel running parallel to the one we occupied.

We stayed for a moment without saying a word. A moment, for us, could mean several minutes, or a few weeks, or far more. According to Myriam, according to what she had explained to us much, much earlier, time around us flowed in inconsistent clumps, without any sense of length, in small or huge spurts we could not comprehend. Her theory was that we had entered not only a world of death, but also a time that moved in these fits and starts and which, most importantly, wouldn't conclude. As we had no idea what she meant by that, she focused on the lack of continuity, on brutal fractures, on the incompleteness of any given moment, long or short. Incompleteness was the only rhythm we could draw on to measure what remained of our existence, the sole way of measuring the interior of this black space. The more she tried to describe in detail the temporal system she had in her head, the less we understood what premises she was working from. She had attempted her explanations several times, then, discouraged, she gave up trying to convince us. However, after a moment, let's say a year or two, or maybe less, or maybe more, we put her suggestions into practice. We did so out of friendship, aimlessness, a shared curiosity. As in our darkness we had no better concrete landmark than that of words, each of us, in turn, proffered a speech. The idea was to invent stories, narracts, to stage several characters from practically nowhere or from our very vague memories and, above all, to see if we could finish our account and contradict the theory of incompleteness that Myriam, our little sister, kept on championing. But our stories, at absolute odds with our wishes, broke off sharply and as if for no reason, and it was impossible to come back to them. Whenever we tried to pick them back up, they would already be torn apart, darkened, and out of reach. Their continuation never came to us and never would. These aren't narracts, Myriam concluded one day in despair, these are interruptacts. We all agreed on that term, and from time to time one of us stopped in our paces, urged the other two to sit, to listen, and once again tried out some words. With very rare exceptions, this pattern of abrupt breaks held.

In this way we have been existing, waiting to leave here, or rather waiting for what had to happen and which could only be extinction.

I focused on looking at what was on the other side of the arrow slit.

— Everything is black out there, I said. There's absolutely nothing to be seen. Maybe it's a second tunnel like ours, or a mass of earth, or a parallel black space.

— Out there where? asked Myriam.

— There's a hole, I said. I'm looking through the hole.

Myriam shifted.

— Where do you see a hole? she asked.

2. Black 2

IN THE VERY FIRST MINUTES and first months of walking in this black space, we hadn't paid much attention to the question of how long our stay would be. Knowing how the time would unfurl was the least of our worries. The most important thing was for us to get to know and habituate ourselves to each other.

Myriam, for example, had long stayed distant and cold. She spoke to us with absolute caution and without ever letting her dismay show. She had to assure herself that she wouldn't be attacked, sexually or otherwise, by the two men accompanying her, in other words by Goodmann or myself, and, in the total darkness in which we found ourselves, it was hard for her to get any sense of what we were like as people. In our lifetime, we had been part of the same organization, but we had worked in different branches and had never met one another. She knew that as members of the Party we had shared the same ethical principles of brotherhood and compassion. But now that all three of us had fallen into a sooty, floating, unforeseen, horrifying world, how could she be sure that we wouldn't, at one moment or another, transform into roving demons, chauvinistic monks, or worse, yet, into obsessive lechers of some sort, into violent, moaning, sperm-swollen semi-humans? I myself had been terrified upon realizing that I wouldn't be undertaking this hopeless trajectory alone. I wasn't afraid about having to fight companions suddenly seized by murderous insanity, because before wandering through the black space I'd actually attained a decent rank in technique, and I was sure that I'd be able, as I once had, to make do in close combat. But what I feared was having to endure the anxious chatter of former colleagues ill-suited to solitude, constantly trying to share their terror, their moral sufferings, and their lack of any future. Having to confront scared people's verbiage was my overarching fear. I suppose Goodmann, in turn, was also worried about our mental or moral fortitude. He had spent the first month in stubborn silence, without ever asking us a single question after we had identified ourselves and the circumstances of our deaths.

Difficult starts. All the same, little by little, we had learned to be together. Once we had overcome our mutual distrust, overcome and forgotten it, we had made for a good group, groping our way forward into nothingness, most often holding our breaths and our eyes open or shut in the heart of these tarry darknesses. We took each other into account and among us a general solidarity, a surly affection between comrades or corpses held sway.

I won't belabor our difficulties in getting used to our new milieu. There were highs and lows, even though the universes we landed in after the end of life are best understood as places where opposites cancel out, and therefore as places where there are neither highs nor lows. It's all pure speculation of more or less illuminated Buddhists, this story of opposites that superimpose, blur into one another, or that no longer exist. The reality is less straightforward. Highs exist as much as lows do, or at least there's reason enough, in our experience, to suppose so. There's no heavenly vault, there's nothing to see, everything is black, but we're very much at the bottom of something when we walk, down a path that stretches onward, a low path, a path down low. We feel it underfoot and not overhead. That's one proof. At the same time, for example, if we want to know what we're walking on, what exactly, it's a perpetual approximation for us. The matter we trample and cross. Sometimes it feels like walking on compacted soot, and sometimes on pulverized slag, or on sand, on a hollow board, on concrete slabs, on plowed dirt, or hard ground covered with moss, or on ashes, or on a muddle of dusty rags, scarves and tatters getting twisted around your ankles and dragging you down for hours or days.

Hours or days.

Here we are. More than the instability of ground, the instability of time and duration were what depressed us. Well, depressed, maybe not, but bothered, yes. At the beginning, as I said, we hadn't paid much attention to that. It hadn't been a priority to measure how long we'd been wandering, certainly not with calendars, a notion that had gone up in smoke once and for all in the shadows' opacity. Once we had grown accustomed to the others' presences, as well as to the strangeness of our progress, we began to measure the time, more out of a retrospective gaze than out of any need to heed some sort of deadline, or maybe out of some unhealthy curiosity, I don't know. Our breathing was too erratic to serve as a benchmark. We might easily find ourselves making our lungs expand and contract for a moment, with some degree of regularity, then stop filling and emptying ourselves and not realize it. Suddenly we might notice that we'd gone meters and kilometers as if underwater, and that our pulmonary sacs didn't care.

In the absence of any other unit of calculation, we could have counted our steps, but such a process would have been strict and besides we moved slowly, often stumbling and taking breaks. Mobilizing our spirits for the sake of numbers disgusted us, and, even when we gave it a try, our minds veered toward topics that seemed less wearisome, memories, speculations on our bodily nature, dives into our own imaginations, or even thinking about the Party's triumph outside this black space and the advent, out there, of an egalitarian, happy society.

Myriam was the one who suggested planting verbal flags in the fleeting, dark matter that the time around us was made of. We could, she claimed, tell stories out loud, and then use those as landmarks. Goodmann liked the idea. In the past, he had done public performances during meetings and conferences, and, like Myriam and me, he had produced several collections of poems and short texts under an assumed name. We would have enough literary energy to round out our turns talking. The idea excited us the more we could see how this was a way to stave off the monotony of our journey. We could count up our stories, I thought to myself, remember their order, and with that draw up a schedule that would measure out the flow of time. And even, in the short term, right now, we could gauge a more compact duration, come back to the notion of hours, half-hours, and quarter-hours, by associating the length of a text with the time needed to recite it before listeners.

Sitting right by one another, knee to knee and almost thigh to thigh, we let Goodmann start us off. He launched into an adventure that promised to include several incidents, a story of a murderer bearing a name quite close to Goodmann's own former one. Edzelmann or Fischmann, I think. I've forgotten. Once his mission was accomplished, the murderer had hopped on a motorcycle and disappeared into the night.

Goodmann's voice was hoarse, as if awash in dust, but he enunciated the sentences with a storyteller's diligence. I was sluggish, comfortably settled into the soot, I could feel the ground's warmth under my rear, or what served as my rear, and I tried my best to stay with the murderer up to the next episode, a meeting with his backer, a new outburst of violence, or a second rendezvous with death, as I noticed that silence was surrounding us. I didn't fall asleep—we experienced stretches of nothingness, rather close to somnolence, but we never slept. And there, instead of lounging on the earth while listening to an energetic anecdote, I was walking down a path that, beneath my feet, was squeaking, as if the road had disappeared beneath a layer of molten, crumbly, resonant salt. It was hot. We kept going without opening our mouths. Not a word, only the sound of our shoes crushing this crackly surface.

— I didn't hear the end of the story, I grumbled after a moment.

— The end, Myriam said. As if that could exist anywhere.

We went on walking, a few thousand paces, most likely. All three of us silent.

— This damn system doesn't work, Goodmann said. Time breaks whenever, however.

— The stories remain, Myriam said consolingly. We have their beginnings, at least, in our memory.

— Yes, at a push, I said. But not what comes after.

— Pfft, what comes after, Myriam said.

— Doesn't work at all, Goodmann said.

3. Korkownuff Something

THE BIG GUY WEAVED between the outstretched bodies. Two or three times, he tripped over legs. The hallway was narrow and badly lit. Almost everyone, even the big guy, was in madras cotton gowns that reeked of dust, interminable meandering, and beggars' food. In the half-light, the big guy had trouble telling cloth apart from skin. When they were trampled underfoot, the bodies barely complained. They moaned to show that they existed and that they had been hurt, but nothing like a sentence escaped their lips.

The big guy ran all the way down the hallway, tapped me with his toe, stopped in front of the door, and let out a sigh, as if he had held his breath for the last half a minute. His hair was oily, the color of a crow's wing, and drops of sweat beaded all over his face. I got up on an elbow to look at him and saw him in detail. His bare calves

20

were dripping as well. His sandaled feet were stained by dirt. He smelled like spicy food, chicken blood, onions. He smoothed his hair and knocked, and, when a voice called him in, he turned the handle, entered somewhat circumspectly, and shut the door again behind him. There was just enough time for me to glimpse daylight in a big room. Then half-darkness encircled us again.

The sleepy wait resumed. Some fellow, whether discouraged or tormented by a pressing need, got up and, after having bumped into several curled-up sleepers blocking the way, he turned right onto the landing and disappeared. Calm settled again. The one hallway light-bulb crackled every so often, growing weak and threatening to permanently snuff its greenish halo. The air was stagnant. I resisted for forty or fifty seconds, then I fell asleep once more.

I had come three days earlier and I had the best spot, right in front of the door. When other applicants had started joining me in the hallway, they hadn't questioned my position. The line had formed silently, nobody was cheating. It now stretched to the ground floor and was governed by instinctive, shared rules. You could step away for a few moments to drink at the tap in the court-yard or relieve your bladder and your intestines; nobody would use that time to move up a few steps and unfairly settle into the spot you'd just left.

Suddenly, I recovered from an instant of unconsciousness. The big guy had just opened the door and was shaking my shoulder using his sandaled foot.

— So that one's already dead? I heard.

I got up immediately, standing at attention in front of the big guy. He and I were the same height and he looked me in the eyes, disgusted. I thought it best to attempt a military salute. Well behind the big guy there were windows and, through them, the blinding brilliance of midday.

— Did he at least bring his file? the big guy asked, predictably enough not returning my salute.

I pointed to the wad by my feet that had been my pillow for more than forty-eight hours. In it was everything concerning my personal data, evidence of life, doctors' letters, veterinary reports, and a few very hazy black X-rays that I'd always considered flattering.

— Get all that mess together and follow me, the big guy ordered.

I quickened myself, hunched down, and traded an apprehensive grimace with the applicant right behind me who'd gotten up as well in hopes that I'd defect and he'd be called up in my stead. As I gathered up my trivial belongings, I noticed some movement in the hallway. The interviews were about to start at last, and that news was traveling from neighbor to neighbor, stirring up tumult and shifts in posture. A sudden desire came over me to give it all up, backtrack, go down the stairs and, once in the courtyard, try to lead a normal existence.

All the same I straightened back up and stepped into the huge room, behind the big guy who walked ahead of me.

— Should I shut the door? I asked in a voice doing its best not to tremble.

I took the big guy's silence as assent and closed the door behind me.

Now I was in front of the recruiting committee. The big guy went and sat with them, wheezing like a buffalo. He had taken my folder, which was already being spread out higgledy-piggledy before two doctors, two servicemen, a psychiatric expert, and the big guy. The doctors and the psychiatrist were wearing white coats, the servicemen were in uniform. Only the big guy was dressed normally, with a white button-up under his Untouchable's gown.

I straightened my back again in what I thought was the position of a soldier who respected hierarchy and I made a basic infantryman's salute twice, the second time very exaggeratedly, almost farfetchedly. I fully realized how clownish I was being. Since I was so sure it would all turn out badly, that knowledge reassured me.

The big guy, on whom I'd fixed my gaze, looked me over disdainfully. The others leafed through the documents painting me in a sympathetic light, revealing my innards and my past, and saving me, for now, from having to talk out loud about myself.

Through the curtainless windows, the sun was strong. It hadn't reached the table where the committee was seated, or the spot where I stood, but it was baking the room, making it a furnace. The two open windows allowed in no air to cool anything. Apart from the big guy, who was melting, my examiners didn't seem bothered by the heat, but I was sure that, under their uniforms, they were soaking.

One of the doctors, turning toward the windows, held up an X-ray, as if to protect himself from the too-strong light, and scrutinized it. His comments unfurled as he kept on examining the photo.

— He's not breathing anymore.

— Eh, his colleague said.

— Have a look for yourself, the doctor replied.

The colleague leaned back and squinted at the negative.

— Looks like it, he said.

The doctor shook the black sheet and it made a flapping sound unlike any other, then he put it back down on the table. He nodded with his next words.

— Who knows if he's ever actually breathed.

I wasn't being asked any questions. The documents went from hand to hand. Nobody suggested that the big guy read or analyze anything. I inferred that his role on the committee was a minor one. He was clearly responsible for walking applicants in and out and, if they didn't fit the criteria, to cut them up in pieces to throw them to the vultures for the ritual of sky burial we had been promised if we were unsuccessful and which, all the same, was what we had always been striving for, apart from being chosen to join the Party, or a cosmonaut team, or worse.

I'd already seen the psychiatric expert, whether somewhere in the camp or elsewhere I couldn't say. I think her name was Médéa Kruntz. She looked up but her eyes didn't stop on me, as if I were transparent or as if my body didn't deserve any such respect. Then she turned to the servicemen.

— If he's skilled at concealment, he's hid it well, she said.

— We don't want him to be beholden to anything, the first officer said threateningly.

— That'll certainly have to be monitored, the second officer said.

I saw that they were all collecting the papers and starting to pass them to the big guy, probably so he could give them to me or burn them. They were thinking.

— I'd propose that we set a probation period, to give him some time to betray or prove himself, said the doctor who had determined that I wasn't breathing anymore.

— A significant period, if so, Médéa Kruntz added.

— All right, the first offer said. He seemed to be the decision-maker. Let's say about fifty years. Then we'll check in with him.

They all fell silent for a second. Now my folder was in front of the big guy. He was stretching a big rubber band around it.

— What's his name again? the first officer asked. His words were aimed at the chubby one, not me.

— Korkownuff something, one of the doctors said. Some unpronounceable name.

— We could simplify matters and just give him another one, the second officer said.

The first officer turned to Médéa Kruntz.

— Might that bother him? If we give him another name?

The expert in human and subhuman occult sciences pursed her lips.

— In principle, yes, that might bother him, she said. But given where he is now, that's not much of a concern anymore.

— Very well, one of the doctors said.

— Hear that, Chuf? asked the session chairman, the officer sitting imposingly right in front of me.

It took me a few seconds before I realized he'd been talking to me. So that was the ridiculous name he'd decided to give me. That appellation put me off completely, but, for the first time since the start of my interview, I felt like a huge step had been taken in my personal journey. Once again, I tried to carry out a military salute, which tipped me off-balance. I just barely got back up.

— He's got it, the officer decided.

Médéa Kruntz looked me over. Her tone was clipped.

— See you in half a century.

The session chairman turned to the big guy.

— You can take him away, he declared.

— Take him where? the big guy asked.

The doctors shrugged together. I saw the big guy pick up my file and lean on the table, then I heard him push the chair back. He stood up.

The light was blinding. The big guy approached me. I still didn't know whether he was going to cut me up in pieces to put me out to pasture for the vultures or whether he was going

4. Fischmann

ABIMAËL FISCHMANN UNLOADED his gun into Bred McDouglas's face, and, paying no mind to the shards of bone and streaks of blood and brain matter now on his murder suit, he left the lodge, shutting the glass door silently.

The night was sweet and starless. A very light rain misted his hair, his face, as he made his way up Schoenberg Street. Not the composer, he suddenly thought. This one was Dardane, not Arnold. Dardane Schoenberg. Maybe this Dardane was a politician, or a minor unknown painter. Or a hero in one of their crappy wars.

Some small-time celebrity barely anyone had heard of. Not the musician.

He turned the corner past the lawns and got into the car that he'd parked under a tree, an acacia. He changed his clothes, taking care not to smear blood on the seats.

Now he had on another uniform and he looked like a biker sitting oddly in the driver's seat of a small car, a Bilma 509 he had stolen a bit earlier and wasn't expecting to get much out of, apart from a way to sneak out of the city. The gas tank was only half full, the clutch wasn't much good, but the engine turned over without any trouble. The rest of the car could be summed up as light brown, with a wet-dog smell, with a rather questionable backseat covered in fur.

The street was deserted, eight hundred meters of more or less dismal emptiness in the rearview mirror, and two hundred meters of damp, dark, low-rise housing ahead.

Fischmann had balled up his murder clothes and stuffed them in a big black plastic bag originally meant for trash, but kept the gun, now reloaded, in his lap. Rather than dash off, tires screeching and pistons firing, he set off as calmly as a family man, following all the rules of the road despite the lack of traffic, turning on his left blinker, pulling carefully away from the sidewalk, only speeding up gradually once he had turned the blinker off.

Once he was on Schoenberg Street again, Fischmann didn't slow down as he went by the house where McDouglas now lay in the sitting room, his head and eyes and cheeks a horrific explosion, his face refashioned into a hideous, unrecognizable shambles. Fischmann didn't slow down as he drove by, but he glanced that way. The front wall was well lit by the streetlights, the windows were dark, including those for the sitting room, which he'd been wise to turn off before going. It seemed like everything in there was asleep, like in all the neighboring low-rises. The varnished wood façade had recently been repainted a slightly bluish-white shade that radiated a message of peaceful, penny-pinching, tacky middle-class life. McDouglas wasn't that sort at all, Fischmann thought.

After a few dozen kilometers, he went past a recycling center, made his way into the darkness of a narrow valley, and came to a stop. In the headlights' glare, the motorcycle he'd left there at the beginning of the night came into view. He opened up the jerrycan that had been banging around in the trunk the whole way over, emptied the gas out under the steering wheel, over the bag of clothes, and on the seats, then, as the 509 caught fire, he strapped on his motorcycle helmet and rode toward Perghee, the blast-furnace region, some hundred and fifty kilometers away.

At first, everything went smoothly, but then the rain started pounding down and, at precisely two-thirty in the morning, came sideways gusts of wind, harsh and impossible to predict or overcome, knocking the motorcycle off balance over and over, and, as he made his way through the town recently rechristened Black Village, he decided it might be a better idea to seek out some shelter than skid around on the potholed road and risk a broken collarbone, or even a drawn-out death in a gulch.

As a hamlet, Black Village probably extended a bit beyond its main street, but for Fischmann it looked above all like a row of dead houses, battered by the increasingly violent rains, with a run-down, unlit gas station at its heart and, at the far end, a motel that was the one place he might possibly take refuge until dawn. A neon sign declared its name—Black Village New Motel—and promised twenty-four-hour service.

Fischmann parked his motorcycle under corrugated-cement roofing and headed toward what might be an office, but was locked and sunk in heavy darkness. Sheets of rain rattled the walls and windows noisily. After ringing the doorbell repeatedly and banging on the door, Fischmann walked two or three minutes down the breezeway that, in principle, protected the doorways of six rooms, protected them from the sun during the day, maybe, but not from the buffets of wind or the downpour. Beneath his feet, the breezeway had become a running stream spangled by raindrops and ghastly dark drumming. The building was deserted, no cars were parked in the lot. For a moment, Fischmann considered breaking one of the locks and plopping down on an armchair or a bed, but he decided it was a bad idea. The motel didn't seem to have a night manager, but there might be an alarm system, or patrols, or somebody watching by camera. He looked up and squinted at the breezeway, the purely symbolic awning overhanging the office, and the post on which the sign glowed. No camera to be seen, but he didn't want to tempt fate. He left the breezeway, braved the onslaught of rain, the water-spouts, the frenzied puddles, and reached his motorcycle, which the cement roofing hadn't done much to protect.

His outfit and his helmet sealed him off from the storm. A diving suit, he thought. I'm getting around in a diving suit. At the bottom of what, of which unimaginable mass of water, he wondered. He'd pulled his gloves back on, he wiped off the soaked seat, he reflected—I could go around to the other side of this shitty building, I wouldn't be right up against this wind, I could find a slightly less gusty spot on the other side of the motel, a spot to wait and maybe even sleep for half an hour, an hour—he was thinking that when suddenly, out the corner of his eye, he noticed movement in one of the rooms' windows.

Someone had opened the curtain and was looking out, right at him. The night and the rain formed a thick, twenty-meter-deep sheet, the outline was blurred by the drops streaming down his helmet, but, even so, there was no question of it. Someone was looking at him.

Fischmann immediately decided that he had nothing to lose in making contact with this unexpected eyewitness. He raised his right arm and waved it as a salute of sorts, in a way to show that he didn't mean any harm, then he went back across the lot and approached the room, once more endured the torrent beneath his feet and the lashing wind and the jostling against his outfit. Then he was back under the breezeway's cover. The figure was clearer now, it didn't move, and once Fischmann was only two steps and a windowpane away from it, he suppressed a jolt and felt something like a wave of coldness deep in his gut. He wasn't the sort to quake in the face of danger, and he'd been in this line of work long enough to handle whatever came his way, but all of a sudden he wondered if maybe it wouldn't be better to jump back and run away as fast as he could.

The drops spreading across the glass kept him from seeing clearly, and the darkness didn't help matters. But what he could be sure of was that he was facing a very white bird, a human-size bird, terrifyingly motionless, staring at him with an impassive, golden gaze, and which

5. Kreutzer

BLOOMKIND SKIRTED THE BUILDING where a lizard farm had sprouted up over the past year, and headed to the veranda of the Party's house, Bloc 2. Air flowed under the dim arch and, as the farm was so close, that air carried the strong stench of a reptilian sty: smaller versions of prehistoric monsters, rotting feed, and crocodilian skins. Grainy, Bloomkind thought. Filthy and grainy.

He crossed the paved courtyard with this insistent impression in his nostrils, powerful enough to distract him for a few seconds from the main topic of his thoughts—Gromov's exclusion from or support by the Party.

If it had been up to Bloomkind, Gromov would have been elimi-nated summarily, in a way that wouldn't have involved the Party at all, for example in a traffic accident, colliding with a tar tank, or maybe, to take another example, in a dust-up by strangers in front of his place who would, afterward, have been branded enemies of the people. Assassins who would have been impossible to identify and track down, Bloomkind thought. But the decision had been made to hear Gromov's case before ejecting him, to give him a chance to mount a defense against this accusation of deviationism, and it was to this meeting of the Executive Committee that Bloomkind was headed.

Once he was past the veranda, Bloomkind found himself in the near-total darkness delimiting the four buildings that made up Bloc 2. Neither the high walls nor the sky let through the least light, no lamp was shining in the rooms visible on this side. There were no reflections in the windows. Should anyone be surveilling the dark depths of the courtyard he would be wholly invisible from behind the glass panes. Bloomkind groped for the door to the stairs leading up to the conference rooms. And, as he thrust his arms out to find the handle, he hit a man reeking of marshes, snakes, and sweat.

He pulled back. His heart raced for a minute from the shock.

— Now, what are you doing there, comrade? he asked in an authoritarian tone that masked his momentary fear.

He stepped back from the other man so as not to have to breathe in his stench.

— Those damn lizards have escaped, the man said. They're every which way now, all around the farm.

— I didn't see a single one on the way here, Bloomkind remarked.

— You don't say.

— Maybe you should look a bit harder, Bloomkind said. There's nothing here.

— This is where I was told to go, the man declared. To protect the Party.

— The Party can take care of itself, Bloomkind said. It's seen worse.

— You don't say, the man repeated.

— And how are you planning to negotiate with these damn lizards? Bloomkind asked.

— With this billy club, the man said.

He held up something, but it was too dark for Bloomkind to make it out.

— Are you in the Party? the man asked. On the Executive Committee?

— Yes, Bloomkind said. Bloomkind of the Executive Committee.

The man wavered for barely a third of a second, then he brought down on Bloomkind's head what turned out to be an iron bludgeon, shattering the skull, then, once the body was crumpled and unresponsive at his feet, the man struck Bloomkind a few more times with all his strength, then set the bludgeon on the ground and dragged Bloomkind over to the trash, then returned to the door, opened it, and started up the stairs. The shadows were even deeper than in the courtyard. He got to the fifth floor, and entered an almost warrenlike set of shut-off, dark hallways, then he came out in a well-lit room and blinked to temper the unexpected inundation of illumination on his retinas.

— Well, someone said. We've just been waiting on Kreutzer. Now we can get started.

Eight people were gathered around the table. Kreutzer went and sat in the empty seat, to the right of Slepniak, the meeting chairman.

— So, Kreutzer, Slepniak said and wrinkled his nose, why are you stinking like a hog?

— Like a lizard, Kreutzer corrected. I had to wait an hour in a spot where there were lizards. They've invaded every part of the area. The farm let them loose.

— Were you waiting for Bloomkind? The question came from Boutrous, one of the assessors.

— Yes, Kreutzer said without skipping a beat.

The entire group was focused on him. As he wasn't adding anything, saying anything, Nochkin, the second assessor, broke the silence.

— And?

— Terminated. The problem's been taken care of. Bloomkind can't pester anybody anymore.

— That pest, said Jabinskaya, the only woman in the room.

— That lecherous lizard, Nochkin said.

Nobody caught the joke, the allusion, nobody reacted, they all furrowed their brows in some way. Silence settled. The group thought about Bloomkind as a political caricature and Kreutzer, in turn, recalled how his forehead shattered, the parietal bones and jawbones he had slammed his nightstick against until all the life was gone from Bloomkind's unmoving body.

— Honestly, you smell pretty bad, said Ulanovski, the regional representative.

Kreutzer grimaced.

— Next time, he said, instead of bothering to dispatch a traitor, I'll take a scented shower so that my comrades don't judge me.

Jabinskaya let out a satisfied laugh.

— What's this whole rigmarole about lizards? she asked almost immediately, so she wouldn't seem useless.

Kreutzer looked her over scornfully. He didn't like her.

— The farm's going down the drain, he said. The director's padding his pockets and he's got no authority. The staff are on strike. The cages were busted open. Those damn creatures got out through the pipes and even the visitors' gate. I had to wait an hour for Bloomkind in a corner of the courtyard where the lizards had taken over to run everything.

— Were they there? Slepniak asked.

— What?

— The lizards? In the courtyard?

— Yes, Kreutzer replied. We fought.

In the seconds that followed, the Executive Committee members' minds were filled with the images of a ghastly battle in the darkness against aggressive, nauseating reptiles with stubborn jaws, hoarse breathing, and swatting tails that inflicted pain and unbearably acidic excrement. Kreutzer, in fact, had swung at random and hadn't tried to counterattack in any way. One lizard had been knocked out right away, the others had scattered, under the veranda, in the stairwell, and who knows where else.

— Now we can talk about the Bloomkind affair, Slepniak said as he formally began the meeting.

As nobody dared to broach the topic, Slepniak took the lead again.

— Bloomkind shouldn't be purged from the party before his corpse has been found, he said. Otherwise we'll be accused of having eliminated him. We can't afford to have the Party's reputation besmirched by such slander at the moment. Let's say that Bloomkind's going through a bad patch, that he's having family issues. A few disagreements can be registered with the Office, but above all we need to let this die out. Bloomkind will be quickly forgotten.

— For starters, his body needs to be found far from Bloc 2, Boutros said.

— Well, someone's going to have to take charge there, Nochkin said.

— Someone actually able to do it, some technical expert, said Simpson, who hadn't spoken up until that point.

— Not me, then, Kreutzer said.

Everyone looked at him with some awkwardness. The act of negatively preempting one of the Party's decisions wasn't something they particularly appreciated, and, because of this one thing, because he had expressed reticence even before the discussion was over, some of them were already wondering if Kreutzer hadn't perhaps been infected by Bloomkind's deviationism. Wondering if Kreutzer hadn't just taken a clearly anti-Party stance.

— I've already done my part, Kreutzer explained.

Slepniak nodded in a seemingly indecisive way.

— Kreutzer, he said. It has to be one of us, otherwise word will get out and we'll have to silence everyone who knows. You're the only one able to do it.

— You started in on Bloomkind, Jabinskaya said sharply. You can finish him off.

Kreutzer shrugged. He would obey the Party, but he would let the silence linger before conceding, maybe because he'd just noticed, in the doorway, a lizard waddling in that was about

6. Clara Schiff 1

I EMERGED FROM UNCONSCIOUSNESS at dawn, or, let's put it this way, at the start of the glow heralding dawn. The landscape was unfurling majestically behind the windows, but not all the shapes could be made out just yet. The sky had rather dark, Prussian-blue tinges that didn't seem all that keen on changing soon, and, although the black silhouette of the mountains on the horizon could be seen and, nearer, the outlines of the bushes bordering the fields, and, nearer still, the vague forms of fog-wreathed horses, there were details missing. I closed my eyes again. I was certain that, when I opened them again, the outside world would be clearer, and, for a few minutes now, I'd been wanting to enjoy what remained of my sleep. With any luck, I thought, I might be able to recall one or two dream-images. I wasn't the only one to have this hope upon waking, this caprice perhaps, even though, most of the time, the memories I had of my dreams were erased thoroughly, instantly, which made my caprice all the more pathetic. As the train brought me the pleasure of being rocked and the wheels' noise was utterly regular, I dozed off once again. No image rose up before me. No image, whether from dreams or my half-consciousness. Just an incessant void that filled with consideration upon consideration on memories of dreams and their appalling operation. After a bout of torpor for some stretch of time I really couldn't guess at, I unstuck my eyelids.

I readied myself to watch the sunrise. For crying out loud, I thought, is this a nightmare or a metaphysical trap or what? Outside, the landscape, rather than being illuminated, had just sunken into darkness. My attention turned to inside the car. Oil lamps had been lit every two meters. The atmosphere suggested that we had entered nighttime, even though I'd held out hope that we were leaving it.

The train's rocking and its wheels' banging continued as it crossed each railroad section, but the spot in which I found myself hardly called to mind a car as it made its way over the tracks, because not only was it not divided into compartments, but it was the size of a huge room in which more or less deep couches and armchairs were comfortably distributed, as in the lobby of a luxury hotel. Light was provided by numerous gas or oil lamps of an outdated style, which exuded a yellowish light that created trembling regions of shadow and darkness. Thick rugs with Mongolian patterns covered the wood floor. Some small wax-finished tables, some chests of drawers, a roll-top desk, and two bookshelves overflowing with leather-bound books. Most of the windows were hidden by heavy ocher drapes and, when they were visible, the murkiness of outside meant they reflected this interior. And nobody to be found, no passenger, apart from me, if I could be counted in this category. I mean in the category of bodies, because, as far as passengers went, I very much was one.

It was when I got up from my seat that I saw the dogs. There were three of them. They were tawny, huge, some mongrel yet powerful breed; they lay outstretched beneath the tables, not far from my armchair, and, with their lively eyes, their brown, gleaming eyes, they watched me. Watched without friendliness. Whenever I made the least movement, they cocked their heads and snarled loudly enough for me to hear despite the metallic noise, the thousands of clicks punctuating the night.

I hate killing dogs. I was taught how to wrestle with dogs, to let them jump at my throat, to escape their jaws at the last moment or push them away, and to catch them by their forepaws, which they don't know how to protect and which puts them immediately at my mercy. I know how to keep fighting with my hands and how to overpower them in a matter of seconds. It's a struggle that I detest. I can dispatch humans without any qualms and in any way at all, some of which are ghastly, and I do what I have to to survive an attack, of course, but any canine's death devastates me.

Very slowly, with small movements systematically followed by a trio of threatening growls, I brought my right hand to my pistol. I could feel a second weapon slung behind me, in a holster, on my belt, and I knew it was the Baikal 442 that I'd stolen off a corpse a month ago. The still-warm corpse of a guy I'd been asked to off, which I'd done without blinking twice. No point recalling the act. I guessed, down to the second, how long it would take the dogs to react once they realized that I'd wrapped my hand around something dangerous to them; it would take them at least three seconds to reach my throat, my wrist, my gut. So what was in my head wasn't the details of my last mission, the origin of this pistol, its technical specifications, the name of its previous owner, the route I'd had to follow before doing the deed. My fingers made their way, centimeter by centimeter. I managed to slip them behind me without alarming the watchdogs, and from that point on I knew there wouldn't be a problem anymore. A minute went by in a stillness that bore no relation to tension. Then I stood up sharply, the Makarov Baikal in my hand, the safety off, and they attacked immediately. Three bullets stunned them in their tracks, and I say stunned because I do think they were, if their gaze was anything to go by. Each projectile went straight through the skull at the forehead. I'm not a bad shot. They collapsed almost as one, stopped in their tracks, and skidded to my feet, as if someone had thrown their hides my way. One of them let out another snarl. I finished him off.

The car now smelled like blood, wild fur, animal breath, gunpowder. And the odor of brain matter was already wafting in the air.

I had no reason to stay there any longer. I stepped over the dogs, made my way between the pieces of furniture in the room, and went into the next room. The doors slid open, there was a sort of air-lock, but no bellows. The roar of the railroad was unabated and, beneath my feet, the ground flickered. Adrenaline was still flowing through my veins, but I was walking unenthusiastically. I didn't feel bad about having shot my attackers rather than having had to tear apart their foreleg joints, amid drool, chaos, and barking, but, even though I couldn't pity the animals or consider myself a murderess, I felt like it had been a shambles. My hands were shaking as if they'd been bitten.

In the next car, I caught my bearings and my breath. Much of what had just happened had been without my breathing. I'd always thought that not inhaling or exhaling might stop or at least deter a metaphysical trap from springing shut, should I have the sensation or the misfortune of being caught in one. A quarrel has raged between scholars on this matter, and each argument they've advanced has struck me as even more ineffective than the last. As for me, I take no sides; when I'm in the thick of things, I simply try not to fill my lungs with air that, especially at the beginning, has to be tainted. Experience has taught me that it's a childish, useless defense. But I force myself to anyway. It's also a way to stay on my toes. And besides, holding one's breath, or barely doing so, makes it easier to aim.

I took a few steps into the new car. It looked like the first one. The drapes were drawn all the way, such that what was outside, the night, the near-darkness, the dark mountains, the dark world, played no further part in this adventure. There weren't any dogs among the tables and, myself excluded, only one presence that was living or close to it could be counted.

Only one living presence. Under the cone of light cast by a huge oil lamp, atop an armchair, leaning against a shelf and sitting cross-legged, an eight- or nine-year-old boy, ten at the most, was deep in a book. What he held was pocket-size and in bad shape, and his eyes were hidden behind small round glasses with utterly black lenses; he didn't express the least bit of curiosity at my presence. I walked up and sat on a couch facing him. The way he was perched on his chair's backrest, he towered over me. I set the still-warm Baikal behind me and looked at him placidly, unaggressively. We stayed that way for a bit, as quiet as two old acquaintances that we weren't, enduring the train's constant rocking, but, overall, not moving. I watched him turn the pages deftly, gracefully, something I'd always admired in humans because, even though my hands are like theirs, they don't allow the same range of movement. They're more powerful and perhaps as adroit, but there's no denying that they're not as dexterous. I guess most onlookers wouldn't notice a thing, but when I have to page through anything that's not a newspaper, I can tell the difference.

— Well, boy, I finally said. What are you reading there?

The little boy tilted his head down to peer over his black glasses. This calm, almost judicial glance was disturbing. In general, I wasn't bothered by the looks humans gave me, suspicious, sneering looks, because they vaguely sensed that I didn't belong to the same species as them. They had been taught to resist their racist instincts, they had been devastated for some centuries now by the shame of pogroms, and now the Neanderthals and the others fraternized easily, but, as soon as they could make out my foreign nature, they startled and immediately, whether or not they mastered the twitching on their face, expressed suspicion, disgust, and hostility. Or fear. They had been taught to fight against the racism their genetics had dictated, but, beneath the surface, their instincts were still there.

The boy gave the impression of examining me objectively and intelligently, and, maybe because of the effect his stillness and his black glasses had, I started wondering if maybe he, like me, wasn't part of the human race.

— Why did you kill the dogs there, Clara? he asked me bluntly.

His voice wasn't childlike, or adult, as if, rather than spoken language, he was resorting to telepathy, or a mixture of the two that rendered the physical dimension of conversation moot.

— Your name is Clara Schiff, yes? Why did you kill them? he asked.

— How do you know my name?

I was surprised and discomfited. He didn't respond. To fill the silence, I pressed the matter:

— How long have you known my name?

The boy shifted slightly. I imagine it was the equivalent of a shrug.

— I've known that for at least three orogones, he said.

Orogones. That was how he counted. So there was little chance he was human.

— Oh, you count in orogones? I said.

— But of course, he said. But why would

7. Sabakayev

THE STREETCAR STOPPED and the driver got out of his seat, stood up, and addressed the passengers.

— Sorry, we're not going any farther. You'll have to make your own way from here on out. Follow the tracks for as long as you can.

Protests rang out, thunderous and sharply worded amid general accursing. As all the tram's sidelights had turned off where it had braked, it was hard to tell who was talking, who had immediately taken the lead. Sabakayev saw one of those leaders in the seat right in front of his. A big guy with squared shoulders, a shaved head, and a far-too-high–pitched voice that we could say, just between us, was like a capon's. He wanted explanations and didn't care about the driver's excuses.

The questions, no matter whether posed by leaders or others, went unanswered. The driver repeated that he was sorry, gesticulated a bit, then slipped in between the control panel and his seat, unlocked the little door up front meant for him alone, a narrow little service door that fell open at his push with a screeching sigh, and, without the least good-bye, he was gone. The night was dense, nothing in the sky shone to light the scene, the lamps were out, and in a handful of seconds, without any further ado, he vanished completely.

The hubbub in the streetcar abated, then rose up again. Sabakayev huddled as best as he could by the window. He wanted to go unnoticed; he pressed a blood-drenched hanky to his thigh and he could tell the hemorrhaging wasn't about to stop. He'd been struck with the broken-off end of a bottle just as he was sure he'd escaped a pogrom that had to still be ongoing in the city center.

The huge shaved head turned his way as it kept on vociferating, evidently searching out some reinforcement, some moral support.

— We shouldn't have let him go, Sabakayev heard. We should have caught him and hung him by the balls.

The man's breath stank of celery, meat scraps, and tooth decay. He seemed to have drunk a basinful of blood.

Sabakayev simply tilted his head down and up without breathing. This tilting was accompanied by a nasal sound vague enough for an idiot to interpret as agreement, but it was too weak. The ill-formed vowel was lost in the brouhaha that still reigned among the passengers and didn't satisfy Shaved Head. He sneeringly looked Sabakayev over a good two seconds, then he turned away sharply, looking for more explicit support elsewhere.

Two passengers got up, and were soon imitated by almost everyone. They fiddled in the darkness with the emergency exit handle. The hinged panels folded open again, and a gust of fresh air invaded the vehicle's interior and reached Sabakayev. Half a minute

later, without much jostling, the streetcar was emptied of its passengers. Sabakayev wanted to stay where he was but, for the sake
of remaining unnoticed, he got up as well and went out. He was
the last one, behind a huge woman with unusually light, extremely
blonde or silvery hair, it was hard to tell in the night.

Sabakayev compressed his wounded leg as best as he could. He
tried not to seem suspicious. All the same, when he set foot on the
ground, he couldn't hold back a groan. The shock of his heel on
the cement had reverberated all the way up his left side. There was
also a measure of surprise in his stifled cry, because the ground was
covered by several centimeters of water. He was sure he'd walked
into a puddle, but, going by the splashing the passengers around
him made, it was evident nothing in this area was dry. If a puddle
could stretch out to the tram's doors, it had to be a very big one.

The woman who had gone before him turned to him. As far as
he could tell in the appalling light, she was Indian, maybe Cayacoe.
Some women from there had survived, of course, but in this part of
the nightmare it was almost a miracle to meet one. Her hair clearly
had to be that white as a result of what she'd endured rather than
her age, since she couldn't be more than fifty or sixty.

She spent almost three seconds looking at Sabakayev from head
to toe, worked out that he was covering up a wound at the top of his
thigh, said nothing of it, and rejoined the group noisily wading away
from the streetcar. The passengers were whining indistinctly here
and there and snorting their fury every three or four steps, as if the
water were too hot or too cold or too deep, whereas it didn't even
come up to their ankles and didn't prevent them from walking. The
leaders for the time being formed a little entourage around them.
They offered short, radical analyses as emergency instructions for
those who, afraid of not having a boss or afraid pure and simple,
were copying their every move.

There were three leaders, each one accompanied by about five people. The rest of the troop, a motley crew of seven or eight individuals, dragged behind. Sabakayev and the Indian woman brought up the rear.

The idea was to follow the tracks nowhere. The metal broached the water's placid surface and sometimes disappeared, hampering the group Shaved Head marshaled by choosing the direction whenever odd railroad switches stymied them.

The migration was heralded by the vehement speeches of the leaders who, over the first few hundred meters, had been keen to ensure their group's sturdy rapport, then, as only Shaved Head had kept on pontificating with his voice like a capon, his quasi-soprano voice squeaking loudly through the shadows, a second leader came to swear fealty and the frontline's numbers were doubled.

A gap opened up between the frontline and the third leader, who had perked up. He claimed to be gathering volunteers to fight against the streetcar company, then, once his verbal delirium was unleashed, he was convinced that he was setting out on a collective battle against authorities on the whole, then against arcane entities responsible for the failure of all organized, intelligent communities, and even the failure of all life, organic or just about. As his speech had grown too abstract and two of his followers had already defected, he came back to concrete goals and suggested that they stop following the tracks and head for a Pakistani restaurant he knew about, and where he was sure they'd take them in and feed them until the night was over.

According to the third leader, the restaurant was nearby, but the gloom was so dense that it was impossible to get any bearing. Apart from the railroad tracks—a pair of gleaming black lines that were less and less parallel, crossed, diverged, reunited with no rhyme nor reason—nothing precise could be made out, especially not anything akin to structures or an urban universe with streets, rows of buildings, and lampposts. The space felt somehow unlikely and there was no way to be sure whether it was infinite, curved, or horridly limited and hermetic.

After fifteen minutes, Shaved Head's group couldn't be heard anymore. So much the better, Sabakayev thought, the fewer crazy people there are, the less crying there'll be.

His left leg was still throbbing painfully, his torn muscles were screaming out their meaty hopelessness. He had lost too much blood and he was starting to fall victim to dizziness. He wanted nothing more than to lie down in the water and die.

The Indian woman next to him took big steps, but didn't show any interest in separating from him. Sabakayev, maybe to better keep her nearby, struck up a conversation.

— In a way, he said, this reminds me of a book I read in prison last year, the story of a guy who missed his train, who walked along the tracks for several days, several weeks, and, after that, underwent a string of adventures, each one more absurd than the last.

The Cayacoe woman didn't seem the least bit intrigued or unintrigued.

— His life went in impossible directions, Sabakayev continued, he went mad, changed his sex, became a monk, got married to a witch . . .

As the Indian woman didn't cock her head to show she was listening, didn't say a word, and kept on going without any shift in whatever her attitude was, Sabakayev fell quiet. He felt stupid. He wasn't much of a talker, he'd tried to be sociable, and, as nothing had come of it, he felt more ashamed than anything. He cleared his throat, and, right then, the pain in his thigh stabbed him. He couldn't hold back his groan and, once again, he decided that the best thing would be to let the Indian woman go off and abandon him, then to lie down in the shadows, in the water, and wait.

— Who did you say he got married to? the Cayacoe woman suddenly asked, as she

8. Demidian

As Demidian stopped talking, the house shook for a second, barely more, with a noise that reminded the three men of an out-of-service elevator banging as it came to an ungentle halt at its resting place, an oily groan, a short echo in an imaginary basement, then silence.

Demidian had been off and away, jabbering as if there were nothing more important than his speech, the final words of which he'd just uttered.

— We're going to go our separate ways and we'll never see each other ever again, he said.

All three of them were sitting in sagging armchairs, and in the center was the low table. Among the wads and piles of hundred- and thousand-dollar bills, the guns lay within easy reach. There hadn't been any worry one of them might be used to cut down on the number of shares, and the men had been calm and professional so far, but each of them knew that it only took the smallest spark to set everything ablaze and that the weapons' presence meant that the apportionment of the loot could change at any moment. In the wake of abrupt, deafening detonations, it could change.

Demidian, for whatever reason, was back to wearing the ski mask he'd worn for the holdup then taken off to drive the van out of town; Escobar smiled with all his tobacco-stained teeth at the prospect of being rich; and McKinley couldn't stop running his freckled hand through his very unruly and very red hair. Chevalier was a bit further off. He hadn't survived the blow one of the two guards had inflicted upon him before Demidian and Escobar had dispatched him and the other guard as well. The base of Chevalier's chin had been dripping since then with what little arterial blood was left, the rest having spurted across his torso and the van's floor, then all over his comrades as they carried him to their hideout in Hound

Dog Creek, then onto the carpeting which was already filthy and piss-soaked, already revolting and badly stained, before his veins finally ran dry.

The silence lasted three seconds and Escobar, even as he kept on smiling with all his ruined teeth, let out a strange giggle.

— So that's how it's shaking out, he said in the same breath as the giggle.

He wanted his two partners to notice that that a disagreeable phenomenon was underway. The cracked leatherette chair he had been lolling in for the past ten minutes had risen up, driven by some incomprehensible force, and was drifting a few more centimeters each second toward the corpse of Chevalier, making such ordinary gestures as grabbing a pistol or a wad of dollars that much harder.

The others looked at him, their eyes boggling. They were clutching the arms of their seats nervously. They, too, had started floating a dozen centimeters above the horrid carpet. Their chairs were gliding, slowly, without any shaking, Demidian seemingly drawing nearer to the table, McKinley by contrast moving away, as if borne on waves toward the TV that nobody had bothered to turn on, the spectacle of all those dollars on the table having sufficed to feed their imaginations.

— Hell, this can't be real, McKinley swore hoarsely. The delicate question of reality and plausibility wasn't one he dwelled on as he tried to get out of his chair.

The chair didn't shift under his movements, as it would have had he been floating on water. McKinley tried to stand, to hoist his body upright, but, as he couldn't get his feet on the ground, he lost his balance and fell forward. In his tumble, he cracked his elbow against a corner of the table. The others heard his yowls of pain, watched him stretch out, levitating above the carpet, and, as he wriggled around trying to clutch and support his broken arm, they felt fear.

— What the shit is this? Escobar yowled, his mouth open in terror like a carp out of water, a carp with uneven, foul teeth.

More out of instinct than any conscious intent, he reached out to the table so he could grab his weapon. All he managed to do was scatter a few thousand dollars. He groaned. The example that had just been made of McKinley's fall was lesson enough: he didn't dare try to climb out of his seat.

It took Demidian a few seconds to catch his breath, the drool in his mouth. With the ski mask back on his face, he looked like a Ku Klux Klan member lost in a parallel universe, a particularly stupid, hopeless member.

— It can't be the police, he said. It's got to do with gravity. It's a gravity problem.

He, too, was trying to master his anxiety. He managed to get hold of his gun before the distance between him and the table grew even more, and he began to think how he was the only one, for now, to feel the comfort of a weapon in his hand.

McKinley, almost by his feet, was still moaning. With each exhale, he let out a keening groan. Out of compassion or some other unclear reason, Demidian stretched out his leg and touched the man's thigh. McKinley stopped moaning.

— What the hell's going on? he shouted. Get me out of this shit!

Likely because he wanted to reassure McKinley, or at least to get him to quiet down, and maybe to reassure himself, Escobar bellowed toward the carpet that they needed to calm down.

— We'll all get out of this, he said. It's just some dirty trick gravity's pulling on us. It'll pass, McKinley. It'll pass.

Among the three of them, for half a minute, there was a spell of quiet. Demidian's voice broke it.

— I don't know what's going on, he said, but it can't just be us. This kind of thing's got to be all over the county, at least. They'll be doing something out there. Just got to wait for help.

— What help? Escobar yelled. What the hell's wrong with you? You want to call the cops? You want the cops to come here?

— I didn't say that, Demidian muttered.

Under his ski mask, he was drenched in perspiration. He had no way to be sure whether it was a cold sweat or the result of the heavy wool.

— Who cares about your gravity, McKinley said.

The three of them were floating around the table, firmly atop nothing, borne by weak, invisible currents in an aimless movement that had them spiraling away from each other and drawing close together, all of it painfully slow. The carpet, freed of the armchairs' weight, was exuding a strong stench of beer, fetor, and rotting synthetic fibers. McKinley's wheezing sometimes masked the anguished breathing of the other two, but not always.

Escobar tried to grab something to get closer to the table and the guns lying there, black amid the grayish-green wads. He did so, rather awkwardly, using the corpse of Chevalier, which itself had risen slightly off the ground. The corpse moved, but was no help in getting him any nearer to the table. Every so often, Escobar lifted a foot, as if to stand up, but he didn't dare put himself into this emptiness that, somehow, wasn't dizzying, because it was at most a dozen centimeters. He preferred to stay on his grotesque pleather raft, in a grotesque position that turned menacing when he stretched out to try to reach the gun on the table.

— Don't try it, Demidian said sharply.

— I'll do what I like, Escobar shot back.

Demidian aimed his pistol at Escobar and was just about to shoot when the door opened and a man, floating as well, pointed his sawn-off shotgun at Demidian's head.

— Do it, finish him off! Escobar said.

The man

9. Bortshuk

As he wasn't fully awake yet, Bortshuk turned on his right side and, without opening his eyes, reached over to inspect the nightstand's contents. Among the things scattered there, he groped around for the brown notebook in which he often jotted down a quick rundown of his dreams, in this way honoring both his affinity for the bizarre and a request made by his doctor, who ran the psychiatry clinic that had tried to set him back to rights after his wife's death, and who was currently treating Bortshuk for a depression he still hadn't extricated himself from.

A ballpoint pen rolled beneath his fingers and slipped out of his grasp for a second. He tried not to focus on his motions so as not to burden his short-term memory with anything that wasn't the images still vaguely floating in his head, or in what lay beneath, or in what served as that. The images, he thought. First the image, then the story, don't think about anything else. He caught the pen and pulled out the notebook, which he had left open on a blank page the night before, then he shifted over onto his other side and got on his elbows in between the sweat-soaked sheets. At the same moment he heard himself letting out a single noisy snore, and he couldn't help but pause and comment on it. He interrogated himself on his likeliest current degree of lucidity: was he or wasn't he still sleeping, was he really handling objects, obeying the instructions his psychiatrist had given him? He saw the psychiatrist Und Gass Hund's office again, and, in a second, the dreamy images that had occupied him were erased. Damn it, they're gone, scattered just like that, he thought. A street, or rather an avenue. Wait, were there trees or not? With half-eaten cars in the roadway. Stuck in the sand. And Monika, there was Monika, young and in a short dress. Her look from the past, from forty years ago. She had just gotten off some sort of streetcar with no windows. Was it night? Already I can't be sure. And what about me? Was I there? That's gone. I'm not even sure it was Monika.

For what it's worth, he thought. Writing down one's dreams. For what that has to offer. For Und Gass Hund to have something to work with.

He finished waking up. Per usual, he had to accept these images' dissolution ruefully. The last remnants were lodged beneath his eyelids. Half of them were already completely made-up or wrong, in accordance with the parasitical work of his intelligence. Monika, he thought. Or maybe someone else.

He opened his eyes. The night went on, but a weak light oozed through the shutter slats, allowing him to make out shapes, and even details in the folds of the sheets. He turned his gaze to the useless notebook and he saw that there was already a text there, five or six clumsily scribbled lines, with uneven letters and strikethroughs. And he was delighted at first, imagining that he'd written down a preliminary dream some hours earlier, in a bout of sleepwalking that he had no memory of. Then his heart jolted: even though the words were malformed by the torpor of sleep, it wasn't his handwriting.

He sat up with a start, his guts seized immediately in a vise of terror, and he swept his eyes across the space.

The room was very dimly lit, but he didn't have any trouble taking it all in and seeing that there was a foreign shape between the window and the wardrobe. It was unmoving and could have been mistaken, for example, for a huge sack of coal, if it hadn't been exhaling all the smells characteristic of a living being: a hobo's old piss-soaked rags with filthy underclothes and more cloths beneath and, further beneath, a plumage that hadn't seen a bath in weeks, grimy skin. In a word, what was between the window and the wardrobe seemed to be a bird built like a furniture mover, wrapped in a nasty, dark-gray overcoat. Bortshuk immediately interpreted its unchanging mien as malevolent.

As he was certain that he'd merely left his nightmares for a horrible reality, Bortshuk pushed the sheets and covers aside, paying no attention to his notebook, and jumped out of bed. At that exact second, his bowels shot out a powerful excremental spray, the instinctive, absurd defense nature had granted him. He heard the diarrhea hit the wall behind him and the stench immediately filled the room, making all breathing, both for the intruder and himself, difficult. Several millions of years earlier, that process had evolved to drive away a predator in the context of an open-air attack, but here, in a confined space, all its shortcomings were evident.

The other being, in the corner, finally showed signs of life. He had just let out a whistle of disgust and had pulled away from the wall to fan his feathers. In Bortshuk's eyes, he seemed to have puffed up; he certainly looked like he weighed more now.

— What do you want? Bortshuk growled.

He had been straining his voice and he had to enunciate each syllable carefully, out of fear that they might shift into an inchoate lowing, the kind he often let out when he wanted to yell for help or put a stop to a dead-end dream sequence. On the whole, he had managed to control the flow of his words, but he hadn't been able to shake off the underlying tremor of fear.

— Well done on that spray of poo, you're a guy who knows how to defend himself, the unnerving fowl remarked sarcastically as he spread one of his wings in front of the window, which only deepened the dimness.

Bortshuk stumbled backward to the bedroom door and tried to open it. It was locked with no key in the keyhole. He leaned against the wood and waited. He wasn't sure how to act now that he had no way out. His heart was pounding wildly. Adrenaline was flowing through his veins and setting his mind spinning rather than suggesting what he might do next.

The two started to fight. The fetors were appalling and shifted with each phase of the battle. Bitterly acidic guano, grimy chicken flesh, beggar's rags, filthy pajamas, drunkard's tatters that had dragged across homeless-shelter floors for days on end, wee-hour breaths, soiled sheets, feathers soaked in perspiration, vile clamminess, blood.

Once the confrontation was over, the bird sat on the bed, towering over Bortshuk's demolished corpse.

— I'd say you gave me a bit of trouble there, he said, almost respectfully.

The truth was that he was more or less intact, if one didn't take into consideration some rips at the top of his overcoat and a few bruises on his legs, because, at one point, Bortshuk had gotten hold of the nightstand lamp and used it to try to break one of the bird's knees.

He didn't need to catch his breath or rub his aching muscles, but all the same he lay back on the bed for a minute, without moving, just thinking. Then he stretched out his limb to pick up the notebook where Bortshuk had archived his dreams. He paged through it, not looking for anything, then he came back to the paragraph he had penned himself, an hour ago, after he had gotten into the room and while Bortshuk was still sleeping like a baby. It was more a way of signing the thing than recounting a dream. He had disfigured his writing terribly, but it was a signature. He always did his best to leave some mark of his passage on paper, and, this time, for this mission, he had felt a pressing need to do so among Bortshuk's laboriously reconstructed dreams. These few lines had also been a sort of brotherly gesture toward Bortshuk, whom he had never felt any hostility toward, not even after he was sent on this mission to eliminate him.

He threw the notebook over his shoulder at the fetid puddle, then he got back up and went to the window. Past the shutters, the dawn's brightness was coming into view, but it barely altered the bedroom's paltry light. He grabbed the window's catch and shook it as a token gesture, since he knew that the window was sealed. In any case, he wouldn't be able to go out that way. His wings weren't strong enough to carry him and the room was too many floors up. He turned his back on the window, stepped over Bortshuk's remains, and walked to the door. He worked the handle and twisted it until it came off. Useless, he thought.

There wasn't much air. The reek and the stench was only growing.

He went to sit on the bed again. He remembered what he had been told before leaving to kill Bortshuk: the shutters won't ever be closed, the door won't ever be locked.

And then he knew he would whisper the words that he had been told to pronounce, that were more or less meaningless to him: Monika? It's done.

He would whisper the line before sinking back into silence and rankness, and, across space, across time, she would hear him.

But for now, he

10. Adlo Tritzang

THE WOVEN STRAW BLIND obscuring the window started flapping. The wind was rising. In the bedroom bereft of all decoration, however, it bore no freshness. What it did bring in from the sweltering outdoors was yet more heat, damp, and bugs.

Sitting in a meditative position, a cushion as hard as wood beneath his derriere, Adlo Trizang was dozing in the stifling night. He looked like a gelong of advanced years, but still in good form, as bronzed and gleaming as a temple statue, and, even though he was dozing, his posture hadn't slackened much, and neither his garb nor his skin were wrinkled. The steady banging of the rod holding down the blind had just put an end to his lethargy. While his thoughts had drifted far from his original goal—which was the silent contemplation of emptiness—he found himself in this cement room, with no decoration whatsoever, surrounded by half-light, steeping in the powerful aroma of coconut oil fueling the little lamp behind him, between him and his straw mattress. Several mosquitoes had landed on his bare shoulder and arms and were relishing infinitesimal quantities of his blood. He let them do so, of course. The irritation resulting from those pricks was inoffensive, and he felt it was rather pleasing to see that in this way he was playing an active role in a vast cycle of animality and reality—vast, ridiculous, and fleeting.

The light wavered, the meditator's shadows danced on the white walls. Adlo Trizang amiably shooed away the flies and creatures flitting nearby and stood back up. The air was searing, the straw curtain was banging convulsively on the window frame. The monk went to retie the knots that should have held the rod in place. A tie had snapped. The curtain trembled like a living thing seized by panic, then calmed down, then almost immediately went on a jag of irrational jolts. It was as if it desperately wanted to get free of its shackles. Through the gaps Adlo Trizang could smell the black breath of the universe, its slowly swelling fury, its already astonishingly damp exhalations. Just another hour or two, and the shadows would be nothing more than spouts, howls, chaos.

The air current was strong in the monastery's hall as Adlo Trizang left his cell. He smoothed out his purple robe, covered his shoulder again. As the back of his fingers ran across his neck he realized he was sweating. The wind was whistling, a familiar sound that he always pricked his ears up for as if it were a harmonic message bearing reasons to live happily in the present. The lamps had been turned off, and he walked some thirty meters in near-darkness, The monks' lodgings on both the left and the right showed no light. Within those, as well, the straw curtains that were the sole barrier between inside and outside could be heard banging. At one point, Adlo Trizang turned around, alerted by the sound of voices. At the very end of the hallway, several monks were making their way calmly to the young monks' sleeping quarters, most likely to make sure that the youngest ones had taken the precautions they'd been told to ahead of a cyclone—closing all shutters, safeguarding books from the water, not getting carried away at the prospect of nature breaking loose.

Adlo Trizang followed Dagdjer Pophen, the superior's plump, beatific assistant, and two expressionless priors, Dondup Djering and Thamsa Rampog, out into the courtyard. All four of them were tasked with fastening the banners' straps, and affixing the handful of windproof panels they had over the openings of the altar most exposed to gusts. More broadly, their job was to ensure the safety of everything. It was impossible to see the sky. The monks groped their way blindly across the especially dark promenade. Dondup Djering went to grab a plank that he knew had to be set in the notches of the altar's doorway, but he didn't return. Thamsa Rampog and Adlo Trizang pushed one, then another cast-iron incense burner safely off to the side. Dagdjer Pophen went to check the prayer wheels along the outer wall.

The wind roared louder. Grains of sand, dust, dried blades of grass, and scarabs pelted Adlo Trizang's face. He turned his head to breathe then faced the wind anew. It brought him deep pleasure to exist, to be able to stand on a land that the unfurious fury of the elements was sweeping thus. And, as he stayed still for a minute, his robe flapping around him, his body riddled by the live and dead debris the night bore, he realized he was alone again in the courtyard. The other monks had withdrawn behind the walls.

He headed to the prayer wheels and set them spinning one by one. They were heavy, and, even in the midst of this whirlwind, they barely moved. Once he had laid hands on each one, he started around again. The sky's darkness had spread heavily across the land, the incessant, swirling whispers surrounded him and kept on pummeling him with darts that were harmless as long as they didn't end up in or near his eyes. As he walked, his eyes were almost completely shut, and when he heard the impacts against his shaved scalp, on his cheeks or arms, he thought he was safe in his skin and that this feeling of security was one of the world's wonders, and that just as wondrous was this capacity to be aware of it. For some immeasurable stretch of time he enjoyed this inner peace as he continued his circular comings and goings past the heavy bronze wheels.

The stretch of time had been immeasurable and, when he emerged from it, at first he swayed on the promenade like a drunken man. The air roared, the darkness was even denser, now leaden with electricity and mist. The rain was very close, a few almost boiling drops preceding it as a vanguard. Adlo Trizang leaned into the wind and clung to the building's walls, the ones dotted with windows. Behind the blinds, several lamps were still burning, but most were out. The monks must have had to blow out the wicks or pinch them off before leaving, along with the young monks, to meet in the shrine room where the superior and his assistants presided. Adlo Trizang counted the openings; his bedroom was the eleventh one from the center door. It was still lit. He went up to it and he peered through the still-flapping blind inside.

The cells all looked so much like one another, the differences being in the position of the oil lamp, or a mandala hung by the doorway, or a slightly more or less faded mattress or cover, or the look of the cushions used for meditating. The differences were also in the occupants, of course, whose physical characteristics were generally quite marked: stoutness, thinness, height, or skin tone.

And Adlo Trizang thought at first that he had come to the wrong window. He was confused for a minute, then that minor uncertainty was gone. Through the straw screen, he had a vision in flickering shadows of his own cell and, clearly visible under the trembling lamp, a monk sat, frozen. This figure, seated in a meditating position, as if utterly estranged from the rest of the world, was perfectly identifiable. Even for someone who didn't often have access to a mirror or the opportunity to contemplate one's own photograph, this being couldn't be mistaken for anyone else. The monk facing him, calmly and seemingly asleep, had to be Adlo Trizang and Adlo Trizang alone.

My twin, he thought, my lost twin. Then he scolded himself for this stupid thought. Still, his serenity was diminished and, without any warning, an unfortunate inner tremor overtook him.

A few years earlier, a guest lama had given a talk on the issue of lost twins, of unborn doppelgängers, of the so-often-unnoticed disappearance of a second fetus in a mother's womb, gone without connecting her physical problems to a false pregnancy—a phenomenon that, according to particular studies, affected one out of eight pregnancies. Adlo Trizang had taken in this information with a sudden nostalgia, as if it explained some of the fantasies that came to his mind deep within his meditations, and which drove him to hope not so much for a merging with the clear light but for a brotherly merging with a being who, with him, would form a new living entity that he imagined tenderly but was never, from a biological point of view, able to define.

He pressed against the blind and tried to push apart its slats. In the cell, the monk didn't seem to be perturbed by the noise outside, the storm's growing roar, the sand pattering against the walls, and now the abnormal movements of the blind that a hand was grabbing and shaking. His eyes were still half-shut, his features wholly impassive.

Adlo Trizang's heart pounded as he let go of the blind and, feeling his way forward, went along the wall up to the building door. He had trouble opening it and just as much trouble closing it again. The entrance hall was pitch-black, everything in the vestibule was turned off, but he knew the way intimately. He headed toward his cell.

When he entered, not unapprehensively, the lamplight was just about to die, but there was time enough to realize that nobody was sitting on the mattress or the cushion he used several times a day and night to repose and reflect. Then the flame sputtered out. The cell was shot through by violent gusts, live or dead insects, and specks of earth. Pine needles slapped him. He tried to revive the flame but without any luck.

Clear your mind, noble brother, have no fear, he thought, a formula used in principle to address a dead soul already on its final trip through a world as impermanent as a bubble. Have no fear, Adlo Trizang, noble brother, he repeated, then he sat on the ground, in the darkness, and shut his eyes.

The rain started almost immediately to pound against the outer wall and with unexpected violence, and he opened his eyes partway. He thought he could make out, in the courtyard, a hand trying to push apart the slats of the blind. Don't let this illusory world perturb you, he thought. Whether it's Adlo Trizang's hand or someone else's doesn't matter anymore. He imagined himself as the monk in the courtyard, as if drowned under a strong wave; he sensed that the other was trying and trying to force open the curtain, and he wondered if his impossible twin

11. Bordushvili

BORDUSHVILI FOLDED HIS WINGS and took shelter on a porch, his back to the wall of the building. His boots had split open and the water seeping in over the last few hundred meters was soaking his feet and gloopglopping unpleasantly with every step. The metal door cold against his shoulder blades, he tried to pull the footwear off so he could empty them out, then let out an exasperated sigh and gave up. Around him, the deluge was unrelenting, horribly noisy yet impossible to see, because the area was deserted and the power supply had been cut off. Not much was visible in the night. A dumb old job, he thought. Just another one.

Over the past fifteen years, the time he had spent in the field after completing training, he had been sent to all sorts of places and finished off a good number of lowlifes, which hadn't bothered his conscience one whit, but, for some months now, a few doubts had been nagging at him. At first, he'd carried out his assignments without a second thought, remorselessly and even with clear triumphalism. He'd been young, he'd had weapons, he'd been fighting for a good cause, and the enemy that kept rising out of its ashes wasn't hard to pick out. The enemy fell into very basic categories, the label he mentally pinned on its corpse left no room for ambiguity, it spoke for itself and it was a radical, summary judgment, a death sentence that none among us would dream of challenging: head of a Werschwell network, pogromist slaughterer, mafioso judge, trafficker of kidnapped children, kidnapper of women and children, warmonger, rapist, torturer, bankroller of calamity, poison-pen propagandist, lapdog of power.

But then, as a reward for the impeccable efficiency of his work, he'd been assigned to a new branch of the Action Center. It was an organ that helmed special missions, not necessarily more technically challenging to organize, but far more debatable, far less transparent on an ideological level. He had been told that the universe's tendency toward apocalypse now needed to be taken into consideration, but more than that, he needed to obey without question.

And so now he was felling unknown figures whose roles in the bleeding quagmire of this world he never managed to nail down. For the last few months, his targets hadn't had the clearly defined profiles of persecutors—sponsors of atrocities, zealous collaborators in the worst sorts of activities. In the instant that he killed them, there was no longer the deep-rooted sensation that had once filled him, of correcting an injustice, of removing some baseness from the prevailing nightmare, of following the supreme morality of goodness. He still did his work without any mistake, dexterously and, when possible, respectfully: he took great care to erase every trace that might give him away or allow investigators to track matters all the way up to the Organization; but, when he withdrew from the scene, he no longer felt the almost joyful relief that he'd experienced in those earlier years. Now when he withdrew, he did so in a bad mood.

A mission was being painstakingly arranged at the Action Head-quarters. Bordushvili had always behaved as a disciplined soldier: he took in and internalized all the information given to him, when needed he requested further detail on specific points, but he never tried to pry particulars out of his ranking officers, never felt any desire to learn more about the hidden reasons for the assassination to come. He didn't question the nature of the tasks assigned to him, and, once he'd done the deed, he gave his report and added no personal comment.

Such comments, however, were something he'd been wanting more and more to articulate, and it wasn't a matter of minor dis-agreements. For example, not long ago, he'd been sent to kill a spi-der. As strange as it might seem, because words like that made the adversary seem at first glance to be negligible, but the assignment had been a delicate one, and had given him great trouble.

To start with, for a week, he'd been given a string of injections and vaccines the composition and purpose of which he wasn't told, but which clearly implied that the situation would be hostile and that the confrontation wouldn't be an easy one. Then the officers had summoned him for a skills test, an ordeal that he was asked to undergo every so often but with a much tighter deadline this time. He had, as usual, overcome every pitfall meant to stymie him, whether physical or mental, on a pulmonary level or a cerebral one. And only then, after those positive outcomes, was he given the confidential report summarizing the work ahead of him. The spider nested at 19 Tambaranian Street but could often be found further down the same neighborhood, in an old, disused Shinto temple. The dossier mentioned that the spider spoke several languages, that it was on the heavier side, and that, on the danger scale that the Organization used as a reference for warning its agents, it was positioned very close to the top, where, generally, martial-arts masters ranked.

Armed with these warnings, Bordushvili made his way to 19 Tambaranian Street and explored the apartment for a long while, leaving nothing to chance and ruthlessly snuffing out anything that might be curled up there as vermin. Arachnids teemed there, as they did everywhere else on the planet, hidden under furniture, in nooks and crannies, deep within cupboards, under the sink, beneath the bathroom pipes, behind wardrobes. After the pale-blue bloodbath, he had to concede that his target was nowhere to be found.

He had left traps everywhere so as to neutralize any intruder and warn him. The equipment the Organization had given him was often falling to pieces, but, among all the instruments he had at his disposal, he figured that a good half of them would be sensitive enough to work should any intruder appear. Then he went toward the Shinto temple and settled there for the night, wary, tremendously wary. He knew that he was setting up camp in a risky area and that his adversary had spotted him. He was counting on the spider's impatience or imprudence to inevitably give away its position and buy him time to react. No matter how violent the confrontation might be, he was sure enough of his instincts to make his way into the very heart of the attack and be certain of immediate preponderance. The night unfurled in silence, or more precisely in the silence of the space, under the eyes of Shintoist deities reduced to variegated wood, while the outside world remained noisy and the street bustling: gusts of wind, dogs barking endlessly, conversations that echoed, arguments, and thrumming engines. The spider hadn't moved, morning was already seeping through the planks sealing the windows, and Bordushvili hadn't received any signal from the traps he'd set in the Tambaranian Street apartment. And so this immobile spiderhunt wore on, this frozen duel, and nothing happened for nine days, until the spider ended up making a move whereupon Bordushvili killed it. He came back to the Center in extreme exhaustion.

On that same Tambaranian Street, ten weeks later, he was asked to murder a faith healer named Attilas Taff. It was a typical mission, but, just as he was doing the deed, Bordushvili had an unpleasant surprise. He had been given a certain amount of information about Attilas Taff, his dispensary, the hours he had arranged for meeting his clients, but he hadn't been told that the man was a monk. Bordushvili, in fact, thought of himself as a monk, and he felt keen sympathy for those whose heads were shaved and whose bodies were attired so. The murder of Attilas Taff was done by the book, but Bordushvili hadn't been able to finish clearing the place, had started grumbling while walking back and forth, and had botched the job of erasing his tracks. He had set the house on fire and fled on foot, in daylight, which, no matter what protocol he was going by, was irresponsible. His superiors hadn't given him grief when he got back, they didn't even allude to it, but, for the first time in his entire career, he'd had nothing to do for a whole trimester. It wasn't outside the realm of possibility that his managers had advised a mandatory break, or taken the time to watch him training at the gym, in the bronze silos designed for flight simulations, and in libraries. And that was when his superiors had reached out again to give him a new job.

A dumb old job, he kept thinking.

He was dressed like a beggar. That was the rule when going to escheated areas, to those neighborhoods strafed by bombs, deep within wretched towns. And that was also his way of respecting the vow of poverty that was one of the Organization's moral pillars, and which extended to the equipment the soldiers used, always at risk of breaking down or jamming at critical moments. Bordushvili let an urge to shiver, then an urge to breathe deeply, pass through him, and, as the drops that a squall was driving down slapped his face and stomach, he clung even more closely to the doorway. The smell of rusting scrap metal filled his nostrils all the way to the back of his tongue. The rain dotted the cobblestones ahead. The storm was formidable and didn't seem keen on stopping anytime soon.

On the other side of the street, he could just make out the small caved-in building his target was sheltering inside. Going by the clues he had been given, he would once again have to execute an odd target, this one by the name of Alphane Gavial. The officers hadn't been able to suss out whether this was a man or a woman, or even some sort of creature more or less connected to the human species. Bordushvili knew that Alphane Gavial weighed less than fifty kilos, was wrapped in rags that billowed out and made it harder to land a hit during hand-to-hand combat, had a fetid pouch, and lived in an inaccessible cement hollow beneath the ruins of that crumbling house not far from where Bordushvili stood. Not to mention that Alphane Gavial was capable of telepathic powers during a fight to the death. And, worst of all, Alphane Gavial thought that humanity was screwed and, contrary to the Organization's preferences, felt that it was time to say so loudly.

Bordushvili took two steps under the pounding rain then drew back and leaned once more against the iron siding he'd momentarily abandoned. The downpour's vehemence had driven him back, as had the idea that he was being sent to execute someone who had the same feeling about humanity and its various components as he himself. It's possible that Alphane Gavial's part of the Organization, he suddenly thought. It's possible that I'm being forced into some petty internal struggle. Why should I

12. Kirkovian

THE RED EMERGENCY LIGHT came on, a nurse rushed into the doctors' lounge, and Kirkovian, who was slipping just then from sleepiness into full sleep, woke and got up. He wasn't clearheaded or ready. The nurse was an unendearing redhead and Kirkovian leveled a querulous stare upon her. The woman got flustered, as if she were besotted with Kirkovian. Her lashes quivered.

— Area 2, she said.

— A pregnancy? Kirkovian asked.

The nurse paused.

— Not really, doctor.

Her name was Paula Djennakis, she was thirty years old, recently divorced, and Kirkovian knew she was living together with an assistant nurse. The surgeon considered her an exemplary professional and ruled out any hormonal or sentimental imbalance as the reason for her embarrassment. Something else was going through her head.

— Is everything all right, Paula? he asked sympathetically.

The woman didn't reply for a second.

— There's a problem down that way, she said.

Kirkovian finished buttoning his white coat.

— Let's have a look, he said. What sort of problem?

They were already out in the hallway. Just twenty meters to the elevator, and then a hundred meters to the operating area.

— The victim doesn't look like anything else, said Paula Djennakis.

— Well, does anybody ever? A smile ran across Kirkovian's face, and then he turned serious again. A factory accident? A biker?

— An alien, Paula Djennakis said.

Kirkovian pursed his lips, then furrowed his brow as if resignedly.

— We've seen our fair share of those.

— It really doesn't look like anything else, Paula Djennakis insisted.

The elevator stopped at the second subbasement. Everything was white, but one set of walls was painted orange. As he always did when the doors opened down there, Kirkovian recalled the meeting where that color had been discussed. He'd voted against orange, against the architect's proposal, and, as usually happened when he was asked his opinion in a democratic context, he'd been outflanked.

They walked without saying a word to the emergency services. At the far end of the hallway, Puccini was coming out of a room, all in blue with a cap over his hair, and he waved at them. He was holding oversized X-rays and, in the quiet, the heavy sheets he was brandishing made that sort of small plastic groan so familiar to that level.

— Never seen that, Puccini said as they got closer.

He seemed more discouraged than wound up. It was hard at times to put up with his humorlessness, but Kirkovian still liked being on a team with him.

Kirkovian stepped into the vestibule to the operating room and scrutinized the light box illuminating what the X-rays had captured. Now several other people, not just Kirkovian and Puccini, were examining the images in silence: two emergency-department interns, two nurses, a stretcher-bearer, and Willmer, the trauma surgeon on call that night, a man Kirkovian had caught snorting line after line of cocaine one night and consequently didn't trust one bit.

For a handful of seconds, everyone was fixated on the black-and-white negatives. The underlings awaited the attending physicians' comments.

— You're right, it doesn't look like anything else, Kirkovian finally said.

— Why do we always get those sorts? Puccini said.

— Gotta wonder what they're here for, Paula Djennakis said.

— Because we provide care free of charge, Kirkovian said with a smile. They don't have that back home.

Things didn't feel so dire anymore.

— So what's happened to our little monster here? Kirkovian asked.

— A chemical burn and some crushing, Puccini said. That's what we were told when he was handed over to us. Nothing else.

— Were the military warned? Kirkovian asked.

— They're the ones who trucked him in, said Albina Trawnik, one of the nurses.

Kirkovian was still looking at the images. He pointed at a hazy blob with tubercular branches that seemed to be surrounded by four sliced-open sea urchins.

— What's that? he asked, not at all bothered by this admission of his ignorance.

— The intermacromial cavity, Willmer said. It's inflating, and it's going to keep swelling because the perilovian tube's ruptured. We'll have to remove it all once we get there. But for now, this is our priority.

With those words, he pointed at something on one of the photos. Kirkovian nodded. Cocaine or not, he had to trust Willmer: he had run a xenosurgery seminar at the Joint Armed Forces Center before tendering his resignation for reasons that remained unclear, but had nothing to do with his competence. Having Willmer on the team that would handle the alien tonight reassured Kirkovian that not everything would fall apart straightaway. Even if Kirkovian would be overseeing the operation, Willmer's knowledge on teratologically altered organisms would be fundamentally useful.

— The military men are already down there, Puccini said. They're in spacesuits and they're waiting.

— We'd do best to do likewise now, Willmer said. I mean, with our uniforms.

With the nurses' help, they suited up as cosmonauts. The protocol for all surgical contact with extraterrestrials was to wear these ridiculous sorts of diving suits.

A shift worker was standing guard at the entrance to the operating room. He didn't stand in the way of the incoming team, but he examined each member with the calculating stare of a serial killer and he didn't stop talking within his helmet, all the sound blocked off so that his top-secret military conversation wouldn't be heard by anyone else. Kirkovian paid him no attention. Nor did he pay any attention to the two army medics standing in the room. He had brought in the X-rays and set them on the light box two meters from the operating table, above the measuring devices. Behind him, Willmer, Puccini, the two nurses, and Paula Djennakis had come in.

On the operating table, the medics had set down a long, transparent tray in which seemed to be several shovelfuls of organs that appeared wholly unfamiliar. If the folds and bumps were anything to go by, the main color was a bluish white or a dull black. This assortment trembled in waves and let out a regular whistle, but it wasn't clear which orifices this noise came from. Between the skins and the transparent walls an almost colorless gel had accumulated.

— I'm going to give it an injection, Puccini announced as he looked over the products on a small medical cart that Albina Trawnik was pushing his way.

— Careful, the first medic said. An injection of what? And where are you planning to stick the needle?

In the time it took to clear their throats once or twice, the eight helmets looked at one another, as in a science-fiction film just when the explorers have realized that a traitor is in their midst.

— Sorry, Kirkovian cut in, his tone brooking no argument. I'm the one who calls the shots here.

— No, the medic replied immediately.

Kirkovian took several seconds to take this in stride and think. Then he stepped back, leaning against the wall by the door and pulled off the top of his uniform. Puccini followed suit, as did Paula Djennakis. Willmer hesitated.

Under the harsh light of the operating-room lights, the alien emitted a noise that seemed like a stretched-out belch, and, when the second medic leaned over it to see what was happening, the alien

13. Theater 1

STAGE RIGHT, IN A CORNER, the phone on the ground rang every so often, though not terribly loudly, such that it didn't interfere with the monologue of the leading man who, seated a meter away, was meditating out loud about his own nightmares and the horrible failure of all humanisms. The device's tinkling played out six or seven times, after which came a long, exhausted silence. The sound was reminiscent of a small, old proletarian bicycle bell and Gavadjiyev, who was also onstage but not speaking, let his thoughts wander far afield of the script and recalled the months of happiness he had shared with the beautiful Marina Gavadjiyeva in Guangzhou, in a time when no engine's backfiring could be heard on the streets and when, at the factories' 6 P.M. close, cyclists in the tens of thousands had swarmed the streets astride uniformly gray boneshakers in a calm frenzy of equally gray and proud outfits, pretending not to care about the cruelty of existence. The monologue continued, the black phone periodically chimed a stammering death rattle, and Gavadjiyev probed deeper into his pillaged, forevermore-lost past. He had no real lines to reel off, and his role boiled down to sustaining his partner's univocal flow with a few brief, rare groans of approval.

The stage was improvised in a warehouse and, beyond the lit area where the two actors performed, the space was violently dark. There was no onlooker. For a week now, despite the poster pinned up at the room's entrance, despite the advertisements on the left and the right of the door announcing that the performance was free, the world at large had shrugged.

The world at large had shrugged. But to say shrug would be sugarcoating it. The first night, as the monologue had already started, three huge burn victims had slumped across the seats in the last row, maybe presuming that the building they'd just entered, one of the few structures still standing in the city, served a medical

67

function. Not having the time to assess the scope of their mistake, they'd let out a few final gasps, then fallen into an almost sepulchral silence. Under the sole lamp at the other end of the depot, a man meant to stand in for all who had borne the brunt of humanity's incomprehensible treachery, done up in rags and, fittingly, wearing the mask of a tall burn victim, was venting his bitterness, his hopelessness, and his philosophy of emptiness in the direction of his associate. That night, Gavadjiyev heard those three audience members come and settle in, and, for the whole of the performance, he'd taken pleasure in speculating on the power of word of mouth that would, no doubt, attract many new theatergoers to this playhouse. He'd appreciated the fact that these three men had stayed without moving, betokening their rapt attention. All the same, their lack of applause at the end of the show had discouraged him, and, once the lights came on after the performance, he had to accept the reality that the audience hadn't survived.

Without any help from the lead, Zababurin, who insisted that he had lower-back problems, he'd lugged the three bodies outside, doing his best to prop them up on either side of the door, setting them in unobscene positions that preserved their dignity. As he did so, taking the liberty of recruiting them to the troupe and, in any case, putting them in a favorable light, he'd slipped cardboard rectangles into their hands with the main details already outlined on the poster: "*Motus, Morituri*, A Tragedie in One Act"; "Starring Bata Gavadjiyev, author, and Sachka Zababurin, actor emeritus"; "Free Entrance Each Night at 9 P.M."

On the following nights, nobody was so bold as to push open the theater door. At first, Gavadjiyev was inclined to lay blame on the three half-burned corpses who, in his thinking, had dissuaded any interested audience members, but eventually, at the moment the lights were turned off, after each performance, he would come out on the promenade side and consider the ruined, night-stricken, terribly silent city, and he would start to think that the lack of an audience was fundamentally rooted in the lack of a surviving population. He was anguished as he took in the smell of ashes and rot that lingered all around and he reentered the warehouse, where Zababurin was sweeping the swath he'd been all too happy to call a stage. The two men had unearthed boxes of cookies and dried fruit, there was a water tap, and as they shared their late dinner, they traded a few words on the drop in cultural-center visits, on how well the performance they'd helmed had gone despite everything, meaning without any lapses of memory or notable incident, then Zababurin went to turn off the power generator block, locked the doors, and the two men prepared to curl up in fetal positions, each in his preferred corner, among the crates and rags that served by turns as a backstage, a green room, and a backdrop.

Motus, Morituri was a play Gavadjiyev had written during some particularly dreary days. He'd composed it among ruins and in the smoke of still-ongoing conflagrations even though everything had already come tumbling down, even though there were no houses or inhabitants or civilizations left to burn. If any critics had survived, they would no doubt have condemned the author for something like an overly caricatural pessimism and a lack of faith in humanity's capability to rise out of the ashes of misfortune, but, luckily for the play's reception, all the journalists and literary tastemakers had, just like everyone else, or just about, been reduced to sooty heaps.

And so the phone rang, not so much interminably as by small stammering iterations. Zababurin continued his monologue, but, that night, he was disconcerted. He broke off here and there, as if he'd lost the thread, or been overcome by such intense discouragement that he couldn't go on. The performance was going awry and Gavadjiyev, after a prolonged silence, decided to get up and pat his comrade's shoulder, then he squatted and answered the phone. At the other end, someone seemed to be stunned by this unexpected appearance of an interlocutor and, to start with, let out a string of gasps, then a brief conversation began.

— Bata Gavadjiyev speaking, said Gavadjiyev. There's nobody left at the number you're trying to reach. There's nobody left anywhere. You've got the wrong number.

— We're coming, the voice said.

In the handset, a click could be heard, then a busy signal, and then another click, and silence.

— It was a wrong number, Gavadjiyev said. And now they've hung up.

— Should I keep going? Zababurin asked.

Gavadjiyev nodded yes and went to sit down again. Zababurin dragged the monologue out for a few more minutes, then fell quiet. They faced one another, unmoving, for a minute. That was the final scene, a mute scene that the director, playwright, and supporting actor had envisioned, but that night, it seemed not to have any end to it.

Just as the power generator seemed to be weakening, two individuals pushed open the warehouse door. In the shadows, it was almost impossible to see who they were, but, as they approached the circle of light, Gavadjiyev realized that they had the shapes of gigantic black urubus swaddled in Organization raincoats.

— Birds, Gavadjiyev sighed to Zababurin.

— I don't care, Zababurin sighed back.

The urubus pulled a bench into the cone of light, a meter away from the actors, sat, and settled in to watch the performance. They'd undone their raincoats, under which their dark-brown corduroy jackets could be seen, as well as their slate-gray pants. Their breathing was audible, as if they'd just completed a difficult task. Gavadjiyev and Zababurin traded a brief look, an expressionless wink, then they retreated into their solitude and anguish.

Nothing happened. The actors were sitting face-to-face in iron chairs, and remained deep in mute stillness. The urubus were comfortable on the bench and breathing loudly.

— You can get on with it, one of the birds finally said.

— The performance already happened, Gavadjiyev finally responded. Come back tomorrow.

The two birds shuddered. One of them reached deep into its raincoat and pulled out something that looked like a brochure in a pitiful state, or rather a wad of loose sheets, some handwritten, others typed up, on which a few photos cut out of magazines had been stapled haphazardly.

— *Motus, Morituri*, A Tragedie in One Act, he read out after having leafed or pretended to leaf through the document. The Organization sent us to hear it.

Zababurin shrugged.

— It's mostly silence, he explained. We face each other and we're silent.

— We came for that, the second urubu said.

— For what? Gavadjiyev asked.

— For the silence, said the second urubu.

— Get on with it, the first urubu insisted sharply.

Zababurin seemed to concentrate, then

14. Marta Bogumil 1

THE CURTAIN STANK LIKE GREASE and a rutting bull's sweat and, when Marta Bogumil lifted it up to enter the store, she struggled not to retch. She especially didn't want the fabric to touch her hair and face. She held her breath as she stepped through, and, as she took a moment so as not to break too violently into this realm welcoming her, which would have made it look like she was aggressive, the heavy cloth fell across her left shoulder and rubbed her cheek and temples. She grimaced and that was the first impression she gave the butcher shop customers: a contorted physiognomy, frenetic eyes half-shut in agony and disgust, a twitching body.

Then she collapsed on the floor strewn with sawdust and ice

water. As the only clothing she had was a shamaness's scarf, she felt the wood debris sticking to her skin, her breasts, her belly, her knees. She must have lost consciousness for a few seconds, because when she started to crawl forward to pull herself back up, she found the butcher had thrown a black rubber mat over her. Then he'd abandoned her to resume serving his customers. He was in the middle of handling a sale for a voluptuous woman attired, like the other people there, in a long felt coat. The lady was dithering over what to buy.

— What's that? She pointed with a hand sheathed in gray wool.

— That's muscle, a nice chunk, the butcher explained.

— And that?

— Torn-off skin. It's very fresh, flayed just this morning.

— Did the animal suffer, at least?

— Nine to one odds, yes.

— Very well. Wrap up two of that for me, then.

— Right away.

In the frame of the backroom door, Marta Bogumil had gotten herself upright again and was wiping off the vile filth stuck to her belly and thighs. She still had the rubber rectangle that the butcher had thrown on her around her shoulders. She tried to put on a brave face, or at least not look insolent. With one hand she dusted herself off, with the other she kept on tugging at the improvised half-poncho with its revolting texture and weight and cadaverous stench. Nobody was looking at her hard and long, but she could sense the furtive glances aimed her way. Past the storekeeper and his customers, on the other side of the window, were tall, monotonous façades blackened by smog on the scale of a mining town. The sky was full of thick clouds, heavy, low clouds. She had reached her destination, but not necessarily the right neighborhood or even the right town. She knew it all depended on how she'd undertaken her trip. Although, to the best of her memory, her trip hadn't gone well. It had stretched out for some number of unusually long hours or years, she'd made her way through long bouts of emptiness, non-existence, and, over and over again, she'd woken up surrounded by strangers huddled around her and staying unnervingly silent when they weren't making biting remarks about her nudity, her bone structure, her chances of surviving in an oily realm, her lung or womb capacity, the ugliness of her internal organs. She had so many memories like that. Nothing was clear and sharp, and the more she tried to focus on the details, to piece together the route and the images, the less her memory worked. Everything was fleeting. Just one isolated scene remained that struck her as so unlikely and revolting that she refused to believe it had happened. But there was no forgetting it. A man was straddling her, pushing apart her thighs violently and penetrating her without asking what she thought, then pulling out and spraying her with disgustingly black semen.

— A slice of liver, another hag declared, her head buried in a dark brown headscarf. From the side where the animal suffered most.

— Right away, the butcher replied immediately.

Marta Bogumil had recovered her spirits. She hadn't crossed the black space just to find herself naked, shivering, and filthy in a shop where blood and flesh and suffering were on sale. She hadn't undergone the lack of duration and light to be set down there, a stinking strip of rubber around her shoulders, in the middle of the moral and physical depravity of slaughterhouse aficionados. She had just one job to do. She had to go and find the shamaness Gordjom, who had gone astray in the worlds between but who had been sighted here, in any case in this area, on Daïtchuud Street or Barabass Boulevard. She had to find her, soothe her if her hell was too unbearable, and help her die if she really wanted to be done with it all.

She let go of the rubber mat. It hit the tiles with a thunk that made everyone in the store jump. All eyes converged on her immediately, as if all the nicely-dressed women were finally realizing that she was there. She scanned the faces: cardboard-like, shriveled-up fiftysomethings who had lived through the worst, undoubtedly in charge of reconstituted homes teeming with obscene, greedy couples, authoritarian women ruling over their clannish troops with an iron fist.

— What about that? one of the women asked, her arm raised to Marta Bogumil.

The butcher shrugged, took a few seconds to pick out a cleaver, and said:

— It's not ready yet, has to marinate first.

In a state of shock, perfectly aware of the meaning of the butcher's words, Marta Bogumil assumed a combat position. Even if her adversary was coming for her with a knife, he had no chance. Even so, she struggled to imagine how he could look at her like an animal that had to marinate in its fear and pain before being gutted and chopped up, and up until this moment she hadn't really believed that she would have to fight to get out of the place she'd landed in. She pulled the scarf tight around her neck, not particularly worried about whether her breasts or crotch were covered. Her nakedness didn't bother her. When one has traveled for several hours or several years in the black realm, one doesn't fret too much about dignity or the appearance of one's body; it's enough, almost a pleasure in fact, to have a body to begin with, and any lack of clothing is utterly beside the point.

The butcher had just asked his customers to leave the store. The five shrews did so swiftly and without a word. Then the man lazily rolled down the iron grate separating the shop from the street and, once the gears had fallen silent, he set himself in front of Marta Bogumil, maintaining a three-meter distance between them that was enough to keep either of them from being caught off-guard. He was holding his cleaver low, and stood at a slight angle. He was breathing from his diaphragm. He looked every bit an ordinary shopkeeper, but he clearly had martial skills.

— What are you doing here, Marta? he asked.

— Have we met? Marta Bogumil responded.

Around her, the smell of soaked sawdust, ruined cadavers, carcasses, hopeless death rattles, and steel all faded away in the unbearable dread of her flesh.

She discreetly adjusted her stance, giving the sole of her right foot an almost undetectable turn. The butcher raised his knife a few centimeters. There was no question that he knew how to fight. He let a breath out through his teeth that didn't inspire confidence in Marta, then he spoke.

— Not yet, actually, he said.

— It'd be nice if you could elaborate, Marta said.

— We've been waiting a quarter century for you, the butcher explained. His voice rang out cleanly. Your name is Marta Bogumil, you have to find the shamaness Gordjom and kill her.

— Not necessarily, Marta protested. Make contact with, but not necessarily kill her.

— Kill her, the butcher repeated. In any case, we've had enough of that bitch. She's an old pest, we've tried to negotiate with her as best we can, but she's slipped through our fingers. We asked for a specialist. That's you. So thank you for coming. You could have come a bit sooner, but we're not going to complain. Thank you, pure and simple.

— The trip here was no walk in the park, you know, Marta shot back.

She slipped readily into this incongruous, deceptively casual conversation, but she was still wary, ready to counter an ambush, unwilling to be lulled by her adversary's words. He could, after all, very easily be a creature from the black space, a twisted monster. She'd been all too quick to believe that she'd left the floating world, reached this area, sidestepped all the metaphysical traps, the darkness, and the slippages between dream and reality, between memory and fantasy, between nothingness and nightmares. And now she wasn't so sure she wasn't in yet another episode of this trip, yet another abominable episode.

— I imagine, said the butcher. But all that's behind you. Now you're on terra firma, on tiles that aren't about to fade away in the blink of an eye. Get a grip, Marta, you noblewoman. You have just about nothing left to fear. Now you can hunt, you can track down the shamaness Gordjom, and you can kill her the way you've learned to, with techniques that we here do not possess. You can help us. You can stay with us on Daïtchuud Street, where the shamaness used to live. We can give you clothes, you can become part of our community, you can marry me so you'll have social status and the freedom to come and go as you wish. You need to have social status to do so and to find the way to the secret residence of the shamaness Gordjom . . .

— Who *are* you? Marta Bogumil cut in.

— But first I'll have to remove your skin, the butcher continued, as if he hadn't heard the interruption.

— What are you . . . Marta said, then took a step back and

15. Oshayana

THE TEACHER'S SCOLDING and the absurdity of the educational requirements had stoked her simmering rage little by little, and, after setting fire to the premises where the literacy classes were held—and where she was the only student—Oshayana had fled into the forest. She was eleven, strong as a horse, and had more than a few tricks up her sleeve.

Biela Bielstein, the teacher, hadn't wasted much time mourning the school's blackened timbers; she'd stuffed a knapsack with provisions and headed off after Oshayana, determined to bring her back home, to rebuild the ruined structure, and to restart her interrupted education from the ground up. The creepers dangled in the humid darkness of the tall trees, and raindrops or chilly sap fell from above, but, down by the ground, there was a stifling heat. Apart from the footsteps and some distant creaking, silence reigned. The birds were few and far between and, barely two or three times a day, Biela Bielstein picked out one flying low among the trees, just as massive and black as their trunks, soundless, almost ghostly, then gone. Even bugs were scarce to be found. Biela Bielstein didn't like walking through the forest, which she had always considered unnervingly calm, but she overcame her bouts of anxiety by thinking about the happiness she would feel once she had found Oshayana. The nights were painful, far too long, and she barely slept at all, overwhelmed by the smell of larvae and marshes that rose up all the more strongly from the earth as if the shadows were fanning them.

After three days, she'd lost Oshayana's tracks completely, but she decided not to give up the search. Conscious that her voice wouldn't carry past a rather meager distance, she didn't call out the girl's name. She ventured in what seemed like the most logical direction, the one that most clearly headed away from what Oshayana had wanted to leave, but, after some time, Biela Bielstein felt like she was moving at random and that she was even going in circles, weaving back and forth, without any direction. But she kept going for another week. Then she decided to retrace her steps. Her provisions, which she had rationed out as carefully as in wartime, were all gone, as was any hope she had of finding Oshayana again.

It took her five days to get back, but she finally reached the village again, which for years we'd called the village: a mere four huts, one of which had been for teaching and was now just a pitiful heap of rubble.

Oshayana and Biela Bielstein were practically the only survivors of a regional anti-Ybür operation that had unfolded across the region; its organizers told her she was the last one. There were two of them. I was the third.

My name is Anassiya Kong. Back then, I was seventeen and, in the village, I didn't take the literacy classes. During the pogrom, I'd first escaped rapists and murderers from the Werschwell Faction, and then those who had called themselves the combers, those who didn't go back to their shacks until one hundred percent of their victims had been mown down, cut down, bled dry. Four months later, I came back to Biela Bielstein's village. I was safe and sound, but I had aged, physically and mentally, at least forty years, I felt like I belonged to the ranks of old women and I claimed that role as my own, and I understood that the human species was far too dangerous for normal folk and that it was best to stay as far away as possible from them.

Biela Bielstein recovered quickly from her fruitless trip into the forest and told me to go follow Oshayana's tracks myself. She was convinced that I'd succeed in finding the little girl, a conviction borne out of her refusal to imagine that Oshayana might have failed in her attempt at independence. She urged me not to take the village into consideration, and to forge onward with Oshayana who, once she'd crossed the forest, might not be able to survive on her own for long and who would try to establish a life in between those towns filled with criminals. I don't know why, likely because she'd seen the girl up close, because she'd sussed out all her abilities despite her bad temper and her unwillingness to learn, Biela Bielstein was certain that Oshayana would be able to take advantage of such a chink in the armor, hide there, and survive there. She asked me to do everything I could, not to give up on my endeavor, no matter how long it took, and, once Oshayana had been found again and tamed again, to help her not to slip into a murderous frenzy, and to be with her at every step, to help her on every day of this new life that would open up before us. She rendered no judgment on the nature of the couple we were at risk of becoming, but she was counting on us to stay together until death us did part.

I bade Biela Bielstein farewell. We knew that we wouldn't see each other again for a very long time and that, in the interim, there would be no way for us to make any sort of contact. We hugged each other tight for several minutes, but we didn't shed any tears. We'd borne witness to such a devastating spate of abominations that, to express our emotions, crying no longer sufficed. I went into the forest and I didn't even bother to look down to follow either of their tracks, Biela Bielstein's or Oshayana's. I went straight, then, after a week, I barely bothered to stick to a direction anymore. In the mornings, I pinpointed the brightest spot that dawn was coming from, and turning my back to it was how I started walking. I'd decided to head west and above all not to change my mind en route. The forest had never appealed to me, I didn't know the names of trees, nobody had taught me how to pick out what to eat. The animals' musk revolted me. Biela Bielstein had told me that, for hundreds of kilometers, I wouldn't run into any wild beasts and very few snakes, at most a few rats and apes, but while I didn't see anything worrisome of that kind, I kept coming across the reek of urine and scat from animals hidden all around me or that my presence had sent fleeing. As I headed westward, I had to bypass several natural obstacles, in some spots dense vegetation that I had to get around, then valleys stagnating with dead water, then rifts in the ground that couldn't be crossed, that forced me to go a long way through shrubby areas and backwater after disheartening backwater. I kept going, perhaps only because I'd hardly come face-to-face with any spiders or millipedes; the few times I actually did, I still had enough space to get away quickly.

I didn't have a specific plan, apart from crossing this arboreal continent and reaching the world Oshayana had taken the risk of entering, then finding her and, after that, never letting her out of my sight again. In the village, we got along well, she agreed to think of me as a sister, but it was true that she'd been plotting her escape for some time, that she'd carefully concealed the plans, and that my first task would be to forge an unbreakable trust between us.

After a month of walking through the half-light, walking that was sometimes broken up by days and nights of heavy rainfall, I came to a plain where the trees were less and less dense, and, as there was a road, I followed it. It led to a town by the name of Dzumgurd. I'd never heard of it and, after so many weeks of loneliness and half-light, it was hard for me to think straight. I didn't know if I'd actually reached a real destination or if I was now in the land of the dead. Dzumgurd turned out to be an unthinkably vast, extraordinarily ugly ghetto. I had no trouble finding a place to stay. I introduced myself as an assistant in an archeology team that had sent me ahead as a scout to determine whether they should or shouldn't come set up a dig here. I guess I played my role well, enough that nobody, even in the administration there, didn't know I was bluffing. Honestly, these people I was now in contact with didn't have much in the way of comprehension skills, and the idea of an academic ground expedition, just when the world was a bloody battlefield, didn't strike them as much more bizarre than anything else. A while later, I dropped the pretense of an archeology team to find a desk job and blend in with the locals. I claimed that I'd lost contact with my sponsors. On that point, too, nobody pestered me with questions. People clearly would rather see me in a normal social situation, a less exotic one than that of scholars who wanted to explore ruins in order to disinter the shameful or humiliating remains of old cultures.

I spent several years in Dzumgurd, with forays into the neighboring and even not-so-near hamlets. I worked at the reception desk for a tapioca factory, since the region produced cassava, and, even as a wage-earner fully integrated into the local economy and, in the eyes of Dzumgurd's citizens, a girl without a past, I never stopped looking discreetly for Oshayana. I had a niggling feeling that the youngster was somewhere close by, and I didn't lose hope, although, among the people I asked, around me or at bars, sometimes in seedy areas that I crept into, pretending that I was an occasional prostitute, I wasn't able to glean any useful information, and there was no sign anywhere of Oshayana or her trace or her doppelgänger or someone who had heard of her.

And then, one night, I was accosted on the street by a drunk or drugged-out beggar asking me point blank if I knew a certain Biela Bielstein. I suddenly felt extremely worried, and under the poor light of a lantern, I tried to make out the features of the woman who'd grabbed my wrist. There was no chance this woman could be Oshayana. I grabbed her arm in turn and gave her the third degree. She had trouble getting her words out, her face was a wreck, and her stench was unbearable. And yet she

16. Fusillade 1

A BULLET HAD GONE through the window, then the muslin curtain with its fly specks and crumbly moths, freeze-dried in their infancy, and then into Klokov's stomach. Time had passed since. Darkness reigned, but now the moonlight made it easier to situate events and actors. The wounded man hadn't lost consciousness. He was huddled down among the glass shards and, leaning against the wall, he awaited his death as he let out brief groans that went unheeded by all, even the gatekeeper's daughter, Natasha, who shivered in anguish and loneliness two paces away.

She was a girl very proud to feel the changes arising in her, but this harsh contact with adult violence had sent her back to the beginning, back into childhood, that murky prison that was child-hood, with the terrible noises and whispers that she had to let out if she wanted consolation. Her father's yells for her to get under the table had been audible; the preteen's silhouette cutting through the half-light, diving, had been visible; her rushing, her slumping were visible; then her movements had slowed. She acted as if she had cut most of the ties binding her to everyone else. She braided and unbraided her thick shock of hair, she clammed up, wrenched her eyes shut. A word, incidentally, about those trembling membranes furrowed by pinkish streaks that betrayed just how violently her hormones were raging. While eating a snack before sundown, Klokov had contemplated those eyes with disgust. They twinkled here and there as if to stun him, a charm offensive that held absolutely no charm or intelligence or modesty. This skin's and even this face's web of veinlets was, in his head, connected with something fundamental, something bothersomely animalistic, and now that he was right by Natasha again, his veterinarian instinct was confirmed.

Pain gnawed at Klokov and she only made matters worse. He grieved as he reconstructed the wheedling back-and-forths and the ridiculous, jostling up-and-downs that had driven him to stop eating his omelet and rush away from the table to stand recklessly in front of the window, in a perfect position for snipers to take aim. At that moment, the girl had stopped all her maneuverings. When the fusillade intensified, she furrowed her forehead, her brows, her entire face. She mumbled, by turns, stupid little melodies and then incantations that had no clear addressee—her dolls, maybe, or her long-gone mother, or unnamable male gods. Once her hair had been tamped down into a dirty-blonde mat, she untied and combed it down, then combed it straight again, then started the process all over again. It took hours. Klokov wanted to hate her, then retched-up blood flooded his mouth. He looked away.

Farther off, the gatekeeper was spewing insults at the attackers, a small group of puppets of capitalism not connected to any of the regular troupes, but who had decided on a lark to put this house and its inhabitants in their crosshairs. He had broken the window's lower left pane and, when he wasn't bellowing, when he wasn't telling these dummies, these lackeys, these sad-sack flunkies what was what, he stuck a rifle barrel through the transparent opening and sent thunder and gunfire into the night, salvos that might have killed and might not have. His brother helped him, copied him, popping up here and there to inundate him with brief, infuriating assessments, proletarian workarounds that didn't incur any deaths, but his main activity consisted of loading weapons. He was half blind so he couldn't be tasked with exterminating the enemy.

All the same, he was a man with a great deal of fighting knowledge, skilled at making his way unerringly among empty casings, cartridges, and breeches. Three rifles had passed through his hands: scalding, black, smoking, perhaps murderous, reeking, greasy, wearying, brown, smelling like powder and saltpeter, maybe ineffective, heavy, powerful, outmoded, vintage, trustworthy, often deployed in their masters' libertarian lives, elegant, unpretentious, inelegant, superannuated, avant-garde, long considered purely decorative objects in union armories, respectfully molten down, lovingly machined by the proletariat of the Orbise mountains, extremely reliable, devoted to the cause, well-maintained, never caught off guard, serviceable, suitable for class wars, imprecise but sufficiently loud to send the enemy rabble scampering, turned silver by the moon's rays, unpolished, gleaming, light. Such was the gatekeepers' arsenal ever since the revolutionary Orbise had fallen. Such was their arsenal and, when the situation called for it, they made use of it.

When the two men weren't battering the enemy's pride, when they weren't tanning the enemy's petty-bourgeois hides and social-democrat heads and breasts and fascist-shit-stained soles with rouge-et-noir words, they talked to each other blandly. For all their bravado, a certain malaise had seeped in.

— Can we or can't we? the half-blind man asked.

— Depends, the gatekeeper replied.

— What if they manage to before dawn? the half-blind man countered.

— Let's not get ahead of ourselves, the gatekeeper growled.

There were also stretches of flight wherein the brothers flapped their linguistic wings, unfurling entire sentences that soared slowly between the kitchen and Klokov's ears before they dissolved in the lunar grayness. Sometimes they could even be heard intoning famous slogans wrought by the Orbise poets. The idea of justified, inevitable, yet unnecessary sacrifice, haunted the snippets of prose and unsaid things on everyone's part. Now that the Orbise was about to be annihilated, only a masochist instinct allowed them to go on leading an existence emptied of all spinelessness, only this suicidal, determined, unbending, admirable masochism fed by centuries-old grudges, drawing its power from ideologists' songs, less instinctive than it seemed, ultimately allowing its exemplars to die upright.

— So long as they don't go insane, don't think, don't turn hell-bent on burning us down, the gatekeeper said.

— Gotta keep 'em from thinking, the half-blind man said as he held out a rifle. They're pea-brains but better not let them put together any ideas. Chuck a few chunks their way for me, why don't you?

The gatekeeper pulled aside the muslin curtain and, for a third of a second, he was in the moonlight and vulnerable. He didn't shift his position as he fired. The buckshot riddled the bushes, the grasses. The raspberry canes whined then fell quiet.

— Too low, the half-blind man said.

Klokov tried to stand back up. He wanted to take part in the fight as well, and he felt far more keenly than he believed that he had some responsibility for the enemy's presence around the small house. They had to have followed him when he'd left Myriyan's residence, or had marked him out when he'd called to give Mimiakin a message. They might have even seen him wiping away his tears as Mimiakin, on the other end of the line, apprised him of Myriyan's death.

The enemy had always been a vile entity in his eyes, a monster to be slain by any means possible, and he couldn't fathom lying low amid these exchanges of hostility, his arms crossed fruitlessly over the centimeters-wide wound that sliced through his guts, as the moon hung above the horizon and the true heroes, the no-name and no-face heroes, spewed onslaughts both of virulent invective and of bullets that were piercing, axing, ramming, pocking, cruel, whipping like fish in water, whistling, perhaps fatal, perhaps barbaric, but deserved, oh so deserved on those followers of the new regime. Klokov sidestepped the avalanche of adjectives and pulled himself upright. Liquid immediately sloshed out of his wound. He could feel carmine depths on his tongue, a flow that was hardly more viscous than saliva but with a revolting taste that commingled bits of hemoglobin and porcini mushroom omelet. Klokov's last meal had been cooked by the half-blind man while the day was dying and, at sunset in the dining room, Klokov hadn't been able to enjoy it. He was fixated on Myriyan's death and he had forced down mouthfuls, paying little attention to the conversation the others at the table were having, the complaints the gatekeeper had about the egg supply status, about the Orbise's downfall, the resurgence of social injustice, the new ascendancy of capitalism, the revival of all capitalism's ignominies, the renascence of man's exploitation by man. As Klokov had reluctantly chewed and swallowed a few bites, the girl had been swirling all around him, brushing up against him, putting on the sorts of lascivious airs that she would have to display at a wedding dance. Suddenly feeling irritated, Klokov had pushed away his plate, pushed back his chair, had presented a three-quarter profile to the window, insisting that he'd heard a voice. The glass and the muslin curtain had offered no protection against the snipers' first shot.

And so Klokov faltered along the wall and then splayed out. His stature was a sailor's, a political commissar's; his robust frame was a light-heavyweight boxer's, a teamster's, a tribune of the plebs. He bravely splayed all that out and held the pose for several seconds, leaning against the darkness, in the balance. He wanted a gun. He mumbled a run of diphthongs that lay bare his intentions and, as nobody responded, he made his way toward the fighting figures, the half-invisible figures of the two brothers.

At that moment a new explosion thundered right by his left cheek, something scraped his gums, and he stumbled into a frenzy of scratches, shooting stars, and now his arms were windmilling, as if he were in a parody, as if he were trying to mime a zombie's oafish stumblings during a storm. The gatekeeper retaliated immediately. Knocked flat by the noise and the pain, Klokov's face was already smashing into the plates and forks and breadcrumbs on the massive slab of wood, cherrywood probably, or perhaps oak. Once he was slumped at Natasha's feet, puking up red and teeth, the girl finally wrenched open her eyes and looked him over. Her eyes gleamed, even in the half-darkness. Her irises gleamed with gold and a tinge of mauve, and slightly askew from minor strabismus which, contrary to what the ladies' magazines insisted, imbued them with no mystery. Klokov met them and was reminded of his wife Myriyan's equally beautiful pupils, which were far darker but just as unforgettably gold-flecked, then he, overwhelmed by nostalgia, shut his eyes. A second later, the girl followed suit.

— Right of the lilacs, there's one out in the open, the half-blind man said.

— I don't see it, the gatekeeper said.

— Just shoot, the

17. With Bouïna Yoghideth

WHETHER UP CLOSE or far off, I'd never seen my cousin Bouïna Yoghideth in flesh and blood. I didn't know the sound of her voice, the smell of her skin, I'd never kissed her cheeks, never hugged her tight, I didn't know how her hair or her clothes or her hands felt against my fingertips. I didn't know what her favorite games were. I'd never whispered in her ear, we'd never had time to become close in any way. For me, back then, Bouïna Yoghideth was nothing more than a face in the background of a family portrait. A face of an unsmiling little girl, a photo that Gramma Schmumm had only shown me once, a family fated to be destroyed. So it couldn't be said that I had, in her life, in our life, ever established any particularly strong bond with her.

All the same, the day my mother told me she had died, I felt a keen pain in my core, as strong as if I had been told, for example, that my little brother was dead. It was as if one of my internal organs had been violently torn out. Something gaped open within me, a horrific void that was in no way abstract, an emptiness that amounted to physical suffering. This pain was immediately followed by a piercing grief that refused to go away. Under the skin of my hands and within my sides I felt perpetual weakness, my tissues clenching, that minuscule tensing one always feels in moments of vertigo, when leaning out of a twenty-second-story window. The pain stayed. The open wound did not heal over, the mourning period did not end. It felt like I had lost a close relative, an irreplaceable friend. That my little brother and our childishness were not gone was no consolation. Despondent, desperate for isolation and silence, I kept thinking about her. When I conjured her up in my mind, I did so with unabated tenderness. I needed her, to have her close by, I pined for her, I couldn't bear not to be able to reach out to her. My sadness was constant.

Soon, however, contact was made between us. Bouïna Yoghideth had found a way to reconstitute herself as best as she could and set foot in reality. She wandered within my dreams. It wasn't, to be clear, a calm, pleasant wandering, and her appearances weren't the respite I had hoped for. In my dreams, Bouïna Yoghideth didn't present herself sympathetically. She was sullen, capricious, talked down to me, second-guessed the truth of my feelings and even my existence, demanded proof of my existence which, in the dream world that we were in, I generally had no way of giving her, or that I gave her only for her to rant grumpily about. I didn't appreciate her attitude, we got into arguments, and when I woke up, my overwhelming feelings were of dismay, anger, and bitterness.

We'd put up a little altar at home in her memory, in the bedroom where repositories of images and statuettes of the departed were kept. I'd taken part in the ceremonies my family had set up there in memory of Bouïna Yoghideth, and also in memory of her parents, who had been killed in the same bomb blast. For a week, each night, we had gathered in front of the images, listened anguishedly to the adults' prayers and eulogies, learning anew about the Ybürs' origins and their determination to persist despite recurrent exterminations, at the same time going over the principles of the global revolution and the revolutionaries' relentlessly radical underpinnings, learning all over again how essential it was to stir up reprisals against capitalists and their servants in life after life. Then my Aunt Vassiliyan, who thus far had presided over the ceremonies as a shamaness or something like it, nailed a red ribbon between the doorposts and hung a vertical banner featuring complicated characters unlikely to be found in dictionaries, handed down from generation to generation solely for writing magical slogans or curses. The room was made into a symbolic space where nothing could enter without good reason.

From that day on, I was the sole member of the family to regularly cross the threshold into the bedroom. Guided by my mother, urged by my Aunt Vassiliyan, I stepped over the ribbon embodying the divide between the living and the dead. I had been warned that this movement wasn't benign, that in entering this unmoving room I was entering an intermediary world where nobody could help me if I were in danger, and my little brother, who had been lectured at length about this, showed no eagerness to follow me. He stayed far away and even refused to accompany me to this empty wing of our home. I'd never complained about his presence beside me, even though we spent most of our days walking together, holding each other's hands to confront adults and the world's horrors. When the time came to take care of my cousin and her remains, my little brother Yoisha disappeared. He had the foresight or the instinct to disappear. I walked alone to the tiny wooden structure in which a shelf bearing my cousin's name, as well as an apple, a cup of water, and a saucer of anti-cockroach pellets had been set.

I was only six years old, and, despite my age, I had been designated warden of the dead.

And so I was the one to light and snuff the candle in front of the altar and I was the one to sing the ritual lines while keeping my eyes fixed on the apple, the cup of water, or the saucer. Very quickly everyone stopped talking me through it, instructing me, encouraging me, holding my hand before I crossed over the threshold. Two weeks went by and they were no longer, not even at a distance, dictating the actions I needed to take, the lines I had to chant, the silences I had to observe. And, after just barely forty-nine days, I was urged to do it all on my own with my ward.

Wardenship is a responsibility that has to be undertaken night and day for at least the duration of one's existence. I carried out my task with a zeal that was sometimes pricked with weariness; Bouïna Yoghideth was a difficult one, she was given to recriminations, and, especially in the beginning, she behaved with me as if I were her born servant. She had trouble letting me be beside her, and the very idea of wardenship, given that we were the same age, was execrable to her.

It took me a long time to steer her toward better behavior, we made our way through bouts of arguing that each of us managed haphazardly and that sometimes brought us to the brink of catastrophe. For a long stretch, we faced each other without saying a word. But then our pairing calmed down. We understood that we were inseparable.

Throughout my childhood, Bouïna Yoghideth was a loyal ally, a wise advisor at all moments, and later on, when I was older, she was a selfless lover, sexually and flamboyantly promiscuous, and, much later on, when it came my turn to wander in other people's dreams, she became a devoted, patient sister, a picture of selflessness.

I'd carried her altar to the house next door, a small four-story building that hadn't been rebuilt or reused in the wake of the conflagrations and, in the silence and stench of dead Ybürs and charred plastic, we spent long afternoons together. Bouïna Yoghideth had dug a hole in the wall. We hid our treasures and a bit of food there.

I think that if someone had gone to the trouble of going down there and doing a bit of snooping in the building's cracks—assuming the building still existed—he would find, at about the level of a child's hand, seashells wrapped in red cloth, a key, the elytra of a golden ground beetle, badges reproducing the portraits of guerrilleros and leaders, anti-cockroach pellets, a star-shaped bit of iron, and a plaque carved out of bone on which Bouïna Yoghideth's name was engraved, along with the exact date of her death in Ybür numerals as well as my own name, with the approximate date of my death, calculated by Bouïna Yoghideth from the motion of the stars and the theory of permanent revolution. I'd inscribed this second date, not without apprehension, as there was no way to be sure what bad surprises fate might still have in store, and I was certain that setting down this number once and for all would result in a nasty end for me. What if I died before then? I wondered. What if I died during a dream, in a world where time was calculated differently? What if the date went past and I wasn't able to die anymore? Under the point of my pocket knife, the bone shrieked. Bouïna Yoghideth insisted, assured me that I had nothing to fear. Go on, she kept saying, write it, make your death sing out with your knife on the dead bone. It'll work, you'll see. And that became a memory for us. We held each other tight, Bouïna Yoghideth and I. The bone screamed out, groaned. I didn't say anything anymore. One of my fingers was nicked, a vermillion drop fell to the ground. Bouïna Yoghideth hunched down, examined the blood and confirmed her calculations thus. I heard her whispering like a little witch. The events that followed were proof that she hadn't been all that wrong, in the end, since

18. Igriyana Gogshog

WE CAN WHINE ALL WE LIKE, but killers simply don't come cheap.

So we have to do the dirty work ourselves.

With all the hassles and risks that entails.

The first hassle: getting a weapon and moving it, then hiding it, while the barracks are teeming with monitors and thieves. The second hassle: the sheer cost of a weapon is almost as ghastly as that of an assassin. For a good gun and its cartridge clip, it'll be some four dollars. Four dollars! Who'd fork over that kind of fortune if they weren't dead set on pulling it off?

The third hassle: what if the target doesn't stay in the line of fire and, on the contrary, fights back by shooting you down?

This was what Igriyana Gogshog was quietly wondering aloud. This was what she was contemplating while doing her best not to fall into the water, as, for some liquid courage, she'd drunk the entire goblet of clear alcohol that the barracks Korean had given her, and now she was having trouble keeping her balance at moments. She walked along the quays and there was no light on the harbor. She ventured another ten meters into the darkness, her short-term goal being a trash bin. Another ten meters and I'll stop behind the bin, she thought. A few more steps and that's it. Her arthritis-ridden and soju-addled legs wobbled. She tried not to stumble over the riggings. Who had the bright idea to moor boats with these shitty huge ropes, she thought. When they're stretched taut, they're like shitty horrible bits of wood, she thought.

I'm too old for this, she thought. Just a few more steps and then I'm done.

To her left, below her feet, three junks bobbed gently and groaned. The old woman could make them out as she squinted into the shadows, but when she didn't do so, she couldn't see anything. She had to rely on her sense of smell, which she hadn't lost despite her elderliness and which, on the contrary, had sharpened over the years. Right beside her, the stench of trash wasn't too pronounced. As for the small boats, they were redolent of spicy cuisines, fish, silty planks, decomposing tar. The prows' lanterns stank with kerosene, but they were all burnt out.

Of course they're burnt out, Igriyana Gogshog thought. No need to help snipers out.

Snipers. No need to help them out.

Well, she thought. If there are any left. They've all flushed each other out. In the end.

A rat scampered slowly past her right shoe, then, as if seized by sudden panic, bolted toward some shadowy hiding place.

In the junks, under the moldering tarps, everyone was asleep. Someone, a grown-up, could be heard coughing in his slumber, in interminable bouts. Not only the basin, but the whole harbor could hear it. There was darkness, the junks' rancid stench, the memory of fuel snaking toward the container, and these lungs ravaged by the enemy's gas or by cancer.

Well, the old woman thought. Nobody's followed me. All is well.

She took another step over one last mooring line.

Nobody can see me, she thought.

Her right elbow bumped against the container. She hiked her skirt up over her stomach, crouched down, pulled off her panties, and let out a long stream of urine. She'd held back a long while, and the resulting experience was so pleasurable that she stopped mumbling, let out a moan, and smiled. Another moment went by, and then she moved away from the nauseating puddle, straightened up, and pulled her clothes back on. Already she wasn't smiling anymore. Now that she had relieved herself, she would make sure the safety on her gun was in the right position.

She stuck her hand down the apron she'd donned when she left, an apron like those seafood sellers wore at market, shiny black, with a huge pocket on the front to hold a knife, some coins, a few bills. Her fingers immediately landed on the metal grip and started toying with the safety's well-oiled mechanism.

Down for instant firing, she recalled. Up to avoid any accidents.

The gun was an eighteen-round Stechkin–Avraamov that a deserter had refused to haggle over when he sold it to her three days earlier, even though he was only giving her four cartridges with it. The old woman knew that she hadn't gotten a good deal, but she had relented, deciding that the soldier could have been her grandson and, given the circumstances, he needed the money far more than she did. When push came to shove, her life was about over and, once she'd used up the little ammunition she had, she could just die. It didn't matter anymore if she spent all her savings on a single purchase.

Her life. It was ending.

Well, my life, she thought. Once I've shot this guy, this Bachuum Dryjdiak, why should I keep doing anything on this earth?

Forty years earlier, she had escaped the third Ybür extermination. She was one of the only people who could claim that honor and, ever since that time, she'd only ever worn black, out of sympathy for the anarchists but also as a signal that she was mourning her people, that she would be mourning her people up until her last sigh.

She went back to muttering, She kept on twiddling with the mechanism on her Stechkin. Down, instant fire. Up, no firing. Down, anyone could shoot. Up, no need to worry.

She repeated the words the soldier had used while haggling. He'd drawled slowly, convinced that she'd never handled this sort of object before. But she had once been trained in the military, and she hardly felt powerless when confronted with the various means humans had perfected for killing one another.

A Stechkin-Avraamov, she whispered. Equipment ushered in right after the fall of the First Soviet Union. Very good equipment. Nobody'd sneeze at it.

Of course not, she thought. Nobody'd sneeze at it.

A humid current from the southeast enveloped her. The wind had swept the docks and the harbor entrance before reaching her. She recognized the mustiness of the fire that had completely destroyed the Aniya Viett refugee camp the week before, reducing the buildings to unkempt carcasses.

Close by, the junks jostled with squeaks and sloshes. The sick man burst out coughing again. It was as if she could distinctly hear his alveolae exploding like bullets and oozing.

What if this cougher's Bachuum Dryjdiak? she whispered.

The fourth hassle: what if, since so many of us aren't really professionals at killing, we come face-to-face with a target we feel pity for? Who, having gangrenous lungs, suddenly no longer seems to deserve the four bullets reserved for him or her?

She moved cautiously toward the quay's edge. The smell of her own urine mixed with the odors of the filthy water lapping down below. She pulled the pistol out of her apron and aimed it at the shapeless mass the three junks formed. The barracks Korean had claimed that Bachuum Dryjdiak would be hiding in one of them but hadn't given any further detail. To kill him, she'd have to look for him down there, in the darkness, amid a welter of shrieks and unexpected gestures, while the little boats were jolted by the rocking, with hardly any way to confirm her target.

The first risk: acting rashly, like the Werschwell Faction's brutes or the imperialist enemy, firing at heaps, slaughtering women and children even as she missed the real target.

What if I waited until dawn? she wondered. With the light I might be able to pick out the silhouettes, the faces.

Dawn. If I waited until then so I didn't stupidly massacre everyone.

Have to pick out the target from the innocent ones, she whispered.

She put the gun back in her apron pocket and pulled back so as to lean against the container. The humidity was audible beneath her soles.

And now I've stepped into my own piss, she said angrily.

She was irritated enough to speak out loud.

— How nice, she said. I'm stepping into my own piss like a hobo.

— Hey you old hag, can't you see when you're about to get your feet in your piss? came a rude voice just beside her.

A man's voice. Or a woman's deep voice. A woman's or a bird's, rather. A human-size bird, in any case. Igriyana Gogshog didn't start, but her heart skipped a beat. The blood drained from her face with an inhale that made her spinster's skin and her skull's bones tremble, and, within her skull, thoughts rose up on two levels. An odd puffin, she thought in the back of her mind. No doubt an odd puffin like in the Ybür legends, a creature without a clear function, who appeared and disappeared without really bringing any comfort to those who needed it. Who appeared at moments of mental ruin or death.

I didn't notice it, she thought more keenly, more clearly, in the front of her mind. It's been watching me from the trash container's shadows. It was watching me when I was crouching to relieve myself.

She still had her hand in her apron pocket. She couldn't decide, and she wrapped her fingers around the weapon, slid her index finger across the trigger, clicked the safety down. Suddenly she couldn't recall which one her gesture corresponded to. Down, she thought hazily. Up. Immediate fire. No. The other way around. With her thumb, she felt around. She couldn't even tell whether the lever was horizontal or not. Her hand was leaden, as it always was when she wasn't sure if she was in a Ybür legend, a bad dream, reality, or elsewhere.

The fifth hassle: what if, confronted by an odd puffin, there was no obvious way to act?

— What of it? she said in a voice hoarse with fear. Don't tell me you've never seen an old girl pissing like an animal.

She'd pulled out the gun and was waving it around unconvincingly at where she thought the voice was coming from. In the darkness, in front of her, nothing moved. She couldn't make out any construable shape. There was some intense silence, then something reminiscent of feathers being smoothed out.

— That's not a gun for you, the other one said. Put it away. Be careful. Click on the safety.

— I'll click on the safety when I want to, Igriyana Gogshog said, her tone ornery.

— Make sure the safety's on, the invisible stranger insisted. Take your finger off the trigger. Shift the lever up and put it away in your pocket.

She still couldn't see a thing. Or maybe a bulge in the darkness, like a huge, black, shapeless mass. Her sense of smell didn't give her any more determinate information. She was too close to the container, the moldering stenches were getting in the way of the fainter avian smell the odd puffin exuded.

— Well, for starters, who are you anyway? she asked.

The other being let a few seconds go by.

— Where did you come from? she asked.

She realized that she was talking, not acting, but she was still unable to make the first move. She couldn't put together her thoughts. Her hand was trembling, more out of frustration than fear. She tightened her hold on the grip. The gun shifted. She clenched it. The weapon was still unsteady.

— Have you taken one to the gut before, ever, in your life? she spat out.

— Yes, it's happened, the other one said.

— Me too, she said, her tone softening.

At that moment, off at the western end of the harbor, by the fuel tanks, a car's headlights turned on and, even from such a distance, the driver's door could be heard slamming shut. The motor's roar, if the ignition had been turned on, was inaudible.

— The police, said the voice. This is when they make their rounds. If they catch you with a Stechkin, you're done for. Hide in the trash.

The second risk: being seized by the police before having carried out justice. Ending up in a camp for illegally carrying a weapon, despite being psychologically prepared for a rogue assassination, and being shot down now or later, after some legal process.

In the distance, the headlights swept slow and yellow across a wall, then vanished. The car must have turned around a building.

Igriyana Gogshog stammered out three or four half-sentences.

He's giving me advice, she thought. Telling me to hide in the container. Stupid advice, but he knows his way around guns. A guy who knows his way around arms, who doesn't like the police, and who didn't take advantage of the darkness to bump me off.

Now, in the night's silence, the car engine could be heard. The thrumming blended into the other silent noises. A new bout of coughing in the junks, the moorings creaking, and, with the rats, a few fleeting squeaks.

— How am I supposed to get into this bin? she asked. It's too high for me, someone's gonna have to give me a leg up.

The headlights weren't visible anymore, and then they were again. The car wasn't simply driving down the quay; it was looping around the depots. It was still far off, but getting closer.

— Figure it out, lady. I gotta go.

— Give me a boost, she pleaded.

— I don't have the time. You're strong enough to do it.

Igriyana Gogshog was still looking at where the voice came from. The headlights had barely altered the depths of the darkness, and yet it was possible to get a clearer idea of how this thing akin to an odd puffin looked, not as the Ybür legends had it, but as it actually was: a beggar's coat that barely hid a wifebeater and a ragged pair of pants, a lumberjack's bearing, a wino's nose, and unkempt feathers. It wasn't so much a figure of salvation as a picture of failure.

The car was getting closer and, while the other being said he didn't have time to help the old woman, she didn't have the time to hem and haw. She gulped down a huge lungful of air as she did when she'd decided to act rashly or talk.

The air was fetid, contaminated with the container's aromas of rotting debris, and it didn't give her the strength she'd been expecting. Even so, she hurriedly stuck her gun in her apron and stretched her arms up to touch the dumpster's brim. Her fingers closed in. So the dumpster wasn't all that tall, after all, she thought. She started shimmying and wriggling with an energy that seemed surprising for someone her age, so as to get herself up to the edge and fall into the trash. The engine was getting louder, much louder than just a minute ago. She could hear her body scraping against the siding, her feet catching hold on the corrugations, the lifting bearings, the crossbeams.

— You'll see if I can't do it myself, you stupid fucking bird, she grumbled.

She righted herself like an acrobat and collapsed just past the siding, hurting herself as she did so.

Now she was curled up inside a dumpster where everything stank like giant's vomit and spoiled fish, she was in the deepest depths of darkness, in some non-place, far away from the world and the police, far from what she'd originally set out for, far from all respectability, and now, at last, in the perfect spot to end a disastrous existence, an overly long, disastrous existence.

She shook herself, tried to find some steadiness among the indistinct detritus, and briefly massaged the spots on her body hurt in the fall: her left knee, her left shoulder, her forehead. There were cartons and preserves jars, but relatively few sticky things. She settled in as best as she could and kept quiet. Once again, around her, the shadows were unwavering. She could hear wings flapping, cloth slapping in the wind, a sigh. The odd puffin was taking off.

Now the police car was nearby. The gravel crunched under the tires, men opened the car doors, slammed them shut. They headed toward the container, toward the junks.

— Hey, one of the voices said. Did you see that?

There was no reply.

— A Stechkin, came the voice again after a few seconds.

Igriyana Gogshog put her hand on her stomach. The gun was gone. It had fallen on the ground when she was hopping over the siding. She hadn't realized it.

The policemen had to be examining their find. They didn't say anything.

— Strange that someone would just leave it there, came one of the voices.

— I don't like it, said the first voice. It has to be a trap. We better get out of here. What if it's a sniper's trap?

— Snipers, the other one said mockingly. They all killed each other off.

— Over time.

— Still.

A moment of indecision went by.

— What about the junks? said the one who had picked up the gun.

— Eh, some other time. Let's just get out of here.

Igriyana Gogshog heard them getting back in the car and driving off. She'd slipped half a meter further down the bin, and she was now more or less sitting inside an old tire and, now, without moving, she started whispering again.

That Bachuum Dryjdiak doesn't lose anything by waiting, she whispered.

The sky above her was obstinately black.

The rubbish she was sprawled across exuded a dizzying stench, but, for whatever reason, she decided to settle in and stay there until morning.

At least until morning, she whispered. Yes, it stinks here, but it's not much worse than the barracks.

— Not much more, she said louder.

She'd raised her tone, maybe to scare off the one or two rats scrabbling around the mess behind her head, but also maybe because her encounter with the odd puffin had knocked her common sense off-kilter and it didn't have all that much sway over her relationship with the world, with space, with words and silence now.

— Hmm, the barracks or the container, she said.

There wasn't any noise anymore on the harbor. At the bottom of this bin, behind the iron sheeting, she was, in any case, walled off from the wood's creaking, the sloshing and groaning of the ropes that were still making a racket but that she couldn't hear anymore. Only the sick man's coughing reached her ears.

— Hmm, I'd go for the barracks, she said.

There was a long stretch of total inaction on her end. She had a feeling that sleepiness was winning out, but she wasn't certain of it, and, all said and told, she didn't care. Every so often, she began murmuring again. She murmured about what she'd experienced lately, about buying the Stechkin-Avraamov, about the booze the Korean had offered her, about the police, and about the odd puffin.

And that guy there, that Bachuum Dryjdiak, she murmured. I have to think about snuffing him out. I have to get something to snuff him out with, and then snuff him out.

I have to rid the world of him.

I have to rid the world of that guy, that Bachuum Dryjdiak.

The rubbish smell was bearable now.

The old woman, in any case, could bear it.

The sky was wholly black, velvety charcoal, without the least glimmer of starlight.

The rats had gone back to their scurrying. They were barely moving.

Don't you try to bite my legs, Igriyana Gogshog murmured. Do what you like in this bin, but don't you bite my legs.

The rats saw to their obligations with some lassitude. They attached little importance to the old woman's presence.

The night wore on.

It's always that, Igriyana Gogshog murmured. Know this: that, no matter what, the night will wear on.

The crime weapon is lost.

The target isn't even in sight.

And instead: sleeping in a trash dumpster.

But at least the night is still wearing on.

— At least there's still that, she said to the rats. The night. There's still that. And besides,

19. With Yoisha

I WAS FOUR YEARS OLD, my little brother one year younger, at the time we were living in the ruins of the Adiana Dardaf ghetto and in a world where, apart from our tight-knit circle, everything was magical and inexplicable. This world was filled with rumors, impressive characters, male or female fighters draped in coats that smelled like smoke and dust, women flitting past like shadows, young or mustached nurses, silent grandmothers and bellowing grandmothers, and amid all that we were supposed to forge the path of our own independence and creature happiness, at the risk, should something go awry, of enclosing ourselves in our childish shadows and no longer moving. The strangers we met on the landing or in the hallways sometimes crouched down to pat our heads or ask kindly questions about our ages, our favorite animals, or the red heroes we most admired. We generally saw them as uncles when they were men and aunts when women, but most of the time we merely deemed them adults, pure and simple, by dint of their adult smells and their way of talking to us as if we were mentally deficient, stroking our scalps while laughing or crying, as some of them were quite emotional, and then abandoning us to deal with something else, as if we had suddenly upset them or as if we meant nothing whatsoever to them. We expected little of these people, but we always kept our affection in reserve and, until they stood back up after having squatted at our level, until they left us, so long as we were in their presence we acted calmly and patiently. We didn't complain when they interrupted our games, we practically stood at attention in front of them to receive their sprays of spit and their embraces, which they assumed were sweet but struck us as rude, and to give serious answers to their bizarre queries.

In one of the bedrooms beside ours there was a place with an iron bed, an iron wardrobe, and a chair, where adults of this sort, uncles and aunts whose names we didn't know or got mixed up, could spend several days without opening the door, except at night when they took advantage of the quiet hallways to wash up and take care of their needs. They stayed as uninvolved as possible in household life, they were rarely to be found sitting at the refectory table or joining the general assemblies. They tried to be forgettable and slipped along walls like shadows and, even if it was the outside world and the street they were hiding from, they lived with us in semi-secrecy. They usually arrived accompanied by my father, who led them through the city via the least monitored lanes and tunnels. They greeted my mother and the women in the house, and the nurses smoking by the entrance, then they went and cloistered themselves in the bedroom where we knew they would collapse on the bed in all their clothes and fall asleep. We had been told not to bother them and to pay them no attention and even, if we were asked about them, to act surprised and insist that we'd never noticed their presence in our house. We were used to obeying the recommendations they gave us, we'd already internalized a number of collective-discipline principles, and, if we were interrogated, we'd have been set up not to know anything further, and therefore not to say anything.

I don't know why, maybe out of some childhood intuition or as a result of some echo of some conversation that had reached our ears and struck us, we'd nicknamed these strangers shootees. The shootees met us in the kitchen, in the hallway covered by old, cracked linoleum, in the front room where we watched the soldiers and nurses playing cards, and, like the others their adult age, they took the time to bend down to us and talk to us kindly. One of them had even gone to the trouble of telling us stories. He was a rather talkative shootee who liked to make jokes and even burst out laughing with us. He reeled off tales about Chapayev, the elephant Marta Ashkarot, the ventriloquist non-humans and humans, about the underground wars, about the trash war, about the war against the rich, about the end of Untermenschen and humanity in general.

I'm unable now to recall his name, but I remember his hearty shootee's face, his gleaming stare, and his flight jacket stippled with naphthous stains and stinking of fuel.

Then one day this short-term guest bedroom went unoccupied and stayed that way. The shootees had changed their habits and, even though they kept on knocking on our door, they no longer slept in our home. My father took them to far-off refuges, they went together down dark paths, they disappeared together for days. My father himself was increasingly absent. We saw the world through a filter. We weren't told about any of this and, when we tried to learn more about the adults' forbidden domain, the nurses scolded us.

There was no apparent change outside, the Adiana Dardaf ghetto didn't seem any more at risk than usual, the streets and the ruins in which we never walked alone didn't reek of burnings and war yet, but, on some level that Yoisha and I were unable to appreciate, the international circumstances had shifted, our concentrational universes were going from worse to worst. Later on, I would learn that the Zaasch group had just been revived and was marching with the Werschwell Faction through the capital. But, at that time in my life, I only saw that the room where the shootees slept was now always empty. All the belongings that piled up there had been cleared out, the only things that remained were the bedframe, with its bare metal base, on which we never sat, and a stool. When we went through the doorway, it felt like we were entering an austere cell where nothing was comfortable or alluring.

That was where we quickly created a magical space reserved for us alone, for Yoisha and me.

We didn't shut the door behind us, because we weren't allowed to, and I also think we were too afraid of being cut off from the world, of finding ourselves isolated in this place that bore the memory of so, so many male and female shootees. But we were now the sole inhabitants of the house to have any reason to go in. We started secretly living in that room, and we developed mysteries and rituals of our own there.

The wall facing the window had been chipped from furniture being moved around, the wallpaper had been torn, and the plaster was visible beneath the rip. We'd opened up the hole by rubbing it with our drool-soaked fingers. There was no question in our minds that there, in that gap, was a deity we had to pay homage to, in one way or another. The deity was named Little Didi. We fed her by pressing mealtime leftovers and spit against the gap. We filled her up unbeknownst to everyone else, keeping it under wraps, because we'd learned that, when it came to particular topics, conversations didn't go well between us and the adults. We had the feeling that the adults wouldn't have approved of our charitable acts. Little Didi didn't appear, but we kept on rubbing her secluded lair with grease and mucus. In the same room a ray of sunlight danced every so often; we hadn't granted it such a divine status, but we maintained rather close relations with it. We called it the Lulette. With the Lulette we got in the habit of playing tag. The game amounted to slapping the spot on the wall or stomping on the spot on the floor where the Lulette appeared, in hopes of seeing her darken and especially slip beneath our hand or foot. She never did. We were just as excited by the food slurry we made to serve Little Didi as we were by our useless attempts to imprison the Lulette. Outside, a bit lower down, tanks went by in long, rigid columns that we finally stopped thinking about, but we never lost track of Little Didi and the slightly less divine Lulette. They were part and parcel of our childhood, we'd never had the least complaint about them, and I'll take this opportunity to share a message with them. If they still exist and if they're capable of hearing my voice, let them reach out to one of us, certainly me as I've survived, I'm here and delighted to trade a few memories of the good old times with them.

And indeed, less than a week ago, I had the chance

20. Fusillade 2

THERE WAS GUNFIRE from the cherry laurels; a bullet shattered a now-no-longer-intact windowpane. Then the metal ricocheted off the lampshade and came to rest in a brick corner. The echo rippled invisibly through Klokov's damp hair, his dusty flanks, his legs overtaken here and there by convulsions.

— What time is it? the gatekeeper asked.

Klokov could hear the half-blind man's words, but they were unintelligible. Encephalic noises got in the way. Within Klokov's temples, his gray matter was pounding, hammering, almost banging panickedly over and over at an emergency exit sealed in pure bone. This phenomenon affected all sounds from outside.

It had to be eleven at night, too far from dawn to pin any hope on it.

The gatekeeper unloaded a new barrage of buckshot in no particular direction. The room reeked of nitric powder made by the Orbise munitions specialists, an unstable, bitter soot so explosive that henchmen's minions and market economy proponents were at great risk.

The half-blind man grumbled about the ammo that would soon need to be rationed out.

Under the table, Natasha was singing an unthreatening nursery rhyme, the same old one. Notwithstanding his negative opinion of the little girl, Klokov could feel a wave of pity overwhelming his depths, a natural sympathy for those who were lost, who would lose everything, and who were afraid. He swallowed the bile ravaging his thorax and he stretched out his arms so as to establish a physical connection with the unfurling yet unhappy, oh so unhappy girl. His hand rummaged through the saltpeter detritus until it landed on Natasha's right ankle. There was a wool sock there fraying around its cuff and altogether rather filthy. Klokov's fingers found nothing tender there.

Natasha might have opened her eyes, might have been terrified not to see the lamplight or moonlight, might have made out a massive, male, huffing mass of muscles. She hadn't paused in her pitiful little song and, as she was certain that someone was starting to grope her, she slid somewhat toward Klokov and propped up her leg the better to move on to the next stage or stages. This stratagem had already slipped Klokov's palm below the unfurling knee. The skirt seemed to be nonexistent. The sock had been relegated to the rank of obsolete accessories. Klokov used his stomach's grumbling as an excuse to pull his hand back. The girl didn't seem offended. She hummed her monotone melody. She had withdrawn anew behind her small, animalistic, autistic eyes: a lost, defenseless being flailing among these horrors and almost crying out, oh absolutely crying out for sympathy. And yet the relationship she was trying to forge with Klokov kept running up against insurmountable obstacles. Through one of the main openings in his face, Klokov expelled a blood-flecked spray into the shadows, then he stiffened in a jolt of non-altruism. He wasn't going to console any old thing anymore. From now on, he was going to deal with his own dysfunction and his own pain.

— It's dying down, the half-blind man said after protracted silence.

— What is? the gatekeeper asked.

— There won't be torpedoes, the half-blind man said.

— Tough luck for us, the gatekeeper responded.

— Aim left of the fuchsias, maybe you'll bring one down.

The gatekeeper fired. In the garden a new attacker slumped, felled in a single blow. A groan of distress lingered in the air for half a minute, then tapered off.

— He's gotten his fill, the half-blind man said.

— How did you? the gatekeeper asked.

— I heard his hiccup. He spun around behind the dahlias. He lay down all bullet-riddled and he's moaning.

— Tough luck for him, the gatekeeper yawned.

In a corner of his frenzied mind, Klokov conjured up an image of this enemy, a man as old as himself, the same weight as himself, the same height, his legs still twitching atrociously. The man had dropped his gun and was curled up on the redolent earth, indifferent to the droplets beading on the dahlias' leaves, indifferent to the dampness, to the grasses' and branches' caresses, the one thing in his mind a fine red dew and the start of a walk down a meat-colored, eggplant-, raspberry-colored beach, the color of a crushed revolution. And then came the rough-and-tumble waves and pain, oh yes, pain.

A respite had fallen. The two brothers conferred in whispers, and did not concern themselves about bothering their guest, Klokov, who was hallucinating beside Natasha's ankles, clinging to avant-garde or semi-human thoughts.

— What do you think the future will be like for us? the gatekeeper asked.

— A ghastly prospect, the half-blind man declared. Everything charred, everything chopped up.

The gatekeeper scowled.

— You could try to think up just one variation, he said.

— There's one, the half-blind man said.

— Well?

— We get out of here, the half-blind man continued. We forge onward.

— How . . .

— We'll have to pay in filthy, filthy lucre.

— But we'll forge onward? the gatekeeper asked.

The half-blind man let out an unclear answer, maybe disapproving, maybe not, through his teeth. The muslin in front of the window billowed with a lascivious swish, the pleats turned menacing, flattened again, danced, and a current that supplanted saltpeter odors with lilac perfume wafted through. Klokov let out a groan and threw up. The night's colorlessness notwithstanding, there was no doubt among anyone present which color predominated in this fluid.

The two brothers fell silent briefly, then turned to Klokov.

— How far along is he? the gatekeeper wondered.

— His third liter, the half-blind man said.

— With the leak his ticker's sprung, why is he even thinking about dawn? the gatekeeper mused.

— He won't keep kicking that long.

They kept talking quietly.

— A sacrifice would calm them down, the half-blind man said.

They're small fry, half-drunk folks letting out their inner animal for a second. They're getting scared seeing so many losses on their end and none on ours.

— You really think it'd calm them down? the gatekeeper replied.

— I say give it a try, the half-blind man said.

— Wouldn't make much of a difference for him, I guess.

— And it'd make some difference for us. It'd push our tough luck back a bit, the half-blind man decided.

— Just have to unload him by the raspberry bushes, the gatekeeper whispered.

— What if it's not enough to calm them down? They've put a price on Klokov's head. Not a very high one, though.

These burbles of conversation ebbed away. In any case, the qualms were there, lurking behind the feverish ideas. Even to save their skin, there wouldn't be any carefree sacrifice of a nearly unknown man, not even a potential hero, a murky ally in this murky battle.

— What about the girl, the gatekeeper sighed. What if we sent them the girl?

— Your words, not mine.

— I'm not sure that'd tickle them the right way, the gatekeeper decided.

They were silent for a third of a minute.

— Just have to unload her by the raspberry bushes, the half-blind man ventured.

He barely had any strength left, but Klokov was tempted to try

21. Yalzane Oymone

A SHADOW SLIPPED BETWEEN two containers and it was a little girl named Yalzane Oymone. She was nine years old and she lived alone. Her home was set up in a third container that nobody even guessed existed, unless they came by sea or by air. But nobody had taken the waterway since the end of the war and, moreover, nobody flew over the harbor area anymore. The birds steered clear of the radiation and the aircraft had stopped slicing through the sky ever since the last battle, which had exhausted all the military resources left on the continent and annihilated an unthinkably large portion of the fighters, their families, and those they were supposed to protect. Ever since that era, which more or less coincided with the death rattle of humanity and was now seventy years past, the world had been quiet. The effects of this ruination lingered unabated; nobody had even tried to rebuild out of the ghetto ruins, nobody had attempted to start up some farming in the countryside, nobody among the survivors dreamed of creating a new civilization, and so the world was bathed in a bland calm that it had never known before, certainly not since the human race had started to stir and crawl across the planet. Now, primordial silence and the steady drip of days and nights reigned anew.

In the harbor, the exploded submarines spat their invisible pollution lazily, assured of being able to do so for a good twenty centuries or thereabouts at the same rate. Time was on their side, even as the regular scrum of wavelets started in on a long, complex process of disintegration. The buildings would ultimately come apart, the flotsam and jetsam would linger and rust in the silt, but the fuel would remain in rude health, as if inexhaustible.

Yalzane Oymone's dwelling overlooked the carcass of the smaller of the two submarines, its name hidden forever under the water and its nationality left undetermined in a time when the idea of nationality was nothing more than that. The little girl called it Uncle Tobbie, and gave the other one, sticking out a bit further off, an identification that she'd read on one of its fins: 7026B-V.

Yalzane Oymone knew how to read. Before collapsing and going black, a young woman had taught her the alphabet and they'd had a bit of time to touch on the complexities of writing. Her adoptive parents had encouraged her efforts by reiterating that she was nine years old, going on ten, and that after they died she would have to face life's many sufferings alone, and that knowing how to read and write would help her. She hadn't argued with them, but in all honesty, the half-century that had followed hadn't brought her many opportunities to practice the art of forming words without saying anything out loud, or the art of understanding them. The books she read were incomprehensible and they were increasingly rare. They spoke of a society, human relations, and feelings that no longer bore any relationship with reality, that had been leveled, and that, set down on paper like this, amounted rather to a mass of absurdities. On the other hand, written language, literary language, overloaded, pompous, stodgy, pretentious language, overly and awkwardly digressive language, inept, abstruse, evasive, allusive language did nothing in conveying information, succeeding only in instilling a terrible din, terrible and badly phrased facts, in her.

The books hadn't given her anything, their pages were burnt or sticky, molten together, newspapers and magazines had kindled her fires for thirty or forty years, until their stock was used up and gone. In any case, no matter what the medium, none of that could answer the question that had nagged at her for so long and that she'd pushed down somewhere deep in her consciousness: why didn't she get any older?

Her physical development had stopped outright before she turned ten. She hadn't noticed any slowdown in her growth, but it had plateaued definitively. Her body hadn't changed any further. Maybe it had grown harder, more resistant, but fundamentally she was permanently a little nine-year-old girl. With, to be fair, a lived experience that had only deepened over the decades, a knowledge that had been shaped by day-to-day difficulties, day-to-day survival, in the face of no future. Yalzane Oymone was now a little girl who had lived a long life as an adult in the post-war silence the oddness of an originally human décor in which all human activity was an event.

An event, but not always a welcome one. Even though the surviving population was rather scarce, Yalzane Oymone had, throughout her existence, met dozens and maybe even hundreds of male and female individuals, but none of them had made a huge difference. She had been raped four times, by men of different ages and in different circumstances, but those four moments all blurred into one another and had all ended the same way: she'd pretended to be open to a second assault and even a long-term relationship, she'd lured her torturers with promises into a place she said was comfortable but was in fact full of traps she knew down to the half-millimeter, and she'd drowned them in creels that they hadn't been able to escape. She'd watched their deaths and, later, after having tried unsuccessfully to cut them up and eat them, she'd thrown them out by Uncle Tobbie so they would turn to tar or be eaten up by the mutant eels and crabs, all this fauna that managed to remain almost completely unseen in these waters that were far from transparent and because of the radiation that altered their behavior, making the new species of crustaceans and anguilliforms suspicious and paranoid.

In terms of language, Yalzane Oymone hadn't regressed any more than the rest of the human species had. Once a semester, she went to the district soviet which, despite its refusal to assume anything other than local responsibilities could have declared itself supreme and controlled the entire continent, as it had no counterpart or competitor for thousands of kilometers in any and all directions. She offered input on harbor matters, on the various problems that could arise in the harbor area she alone inhabited. Other area spokespeople piped up in turn. These conversations were difficult, gravelly, it became clear that there was a gulf between what they had contemplated for months in solitude and what suddenly, obscenely, escaped their lips in front of an audience. The gatherings boiled down to some fifteen people, usually fat, sick women with sullen, dust-stained faces, or hags. Every so often a fortysomething man went to the trouble of leaving his secret hideaway to complain and bemoan how things in the world had gone to seed and how his cancer was worsening. The males were unnerving, they weren't courageous or outspoken, they betokened a barely concealed brutishness that could break out at any moment, but Yalzane Oymone managed to scare them away with her retorts and the witchlike aspect of her eternal youth. All things considered, only having been sexually attacked by four people over seventy years was testament to her ability to command respect from the anthropoid refuse that the last representatives of the species were. Certainly far more than the women, the forty-something men were the very figure of exhaustion and unhappiness. Nobody knew how or when they had been birthed, long after the devastation, and they were filled with the bitterness and disgust of living. Sentiments that could have amounted to, for example, pity never entered Yalzane Oymone's imagination, but even so it gave her no joy to realize that they were easy to manipulate and over-power intellectually. Most of them, deep down, were fearful animals swiftly borne away by death. That gave her no fear.

I met Yalzane Oymone three years ago, when I was sent into the region for an execution. Upon touching ground there, I quickly understood that the geographical markers, the layout of the streets, the traces of the waterways didn't match up to what was on the map the Organization had pieced together from guesswork after the apocalypse's last paroxysms. I had to track down and eliminate a creature named Djonaze Milwaukee, who was neither man nor woman, claiming to have achieved immortality and having amassed a group of cannibals. The Organization didn't condemn cannibalism anymore, it barely interfered with human affairs, deeming human-ity's extinction imminent, but it had detected a danger of some sort in Djonaze Milwaukee that I was to root out completely. I had been lost in the labyrinth of ruins and come out on the harbor, and it was on that day, at sunset, that I saw a shadow slip between two containers, the astonishing silhouette of a little girl who I didn't yet know was named Yalzane Oymone.

I'll describe later how I found and assassinated Djonaze Milwaukee and the leader's nine disciples. Suffice it to say that the task entrusted to me could have been less ignominious. Once it was dealt with, the process of returning to the Organization was hampered by a succession of geomagnetic storms and I was informed that the transfer was delayed indefinitely. I'm still waiting for the wheels, if they can be called that, to be set in motion. I'm waiting while making a home for myself on the harbor, not far from Yalzane Oymone's lodgings, by the submarines with their batteries and warheads inexorably exuding an odorless, noiseless death.

As for Yalzane Oymone, I learned many things over three years, but the first thing I should say is that

22. Marta Bogumil 2

THE PATH SLOPED GENTLY downward through the countryside. It was nice out, the sun peeked anxiously through a uniformly gray sheet of clouds, and, even if the sky wasn't an intensely azure blue, it was still breathtaking. Marta Bogumil pushed open the gate, shut it behind her, and entered a meadow where huge, seemingly clumsy horses were grazing; they evoked not so much elegant races or stampedes, or even plowing, as glue factories. The creatures were wreathed in fleas and smelled like manure and sweat. Marta went past them without stroking their rumps or speaking to them. The insects accompanied her for another fifty meters or so. She swatted them away angrily even as she realized that doing so only broadened the sphere of exhalation and flesh so attractive to them. A horsefly landed right by her left eye and, at that exact second, as if driven by an urgent need, it administered a painful sting. She associated horsefly stings with filth and tetanus and she started to wish she hadn't taken this shortcut instead of the asphalt road that, frankly, would have forced her to spend another half hour wilting in the heat before finally reaching the colony. She did need to conserve her strength. A heavy backpack was slung across her shoulders, she was seven months pregnant, and she wasn't sure she'd be able to get through the hardest spots, especially the one where she'd have to explain herself to the welcome committee.

A shrew bolted in front of her feet and immediately disappeared among the sagebrush. Marta stopped momentarily in hopes of catching sight of the small creature, whose existence touched her, beneath the leaves, but she didn't see anything. The air above the grasses was humming, the meadow exhaled the scents of midsummer. The fleas didn't bother her anymore. She checked again to make sure the shrew had no intention of making itself seen, then she went back on her way. She only had three hundred meters or so to go before reaching the fence.

She opened the service gate and came out onto the road. On the other side of the gully, stretching out toward the horizon, was a succession of heavy-duty or wooden buildings, some of which had an upstairs. The penal colony looked rather like an infinite city: very gray, very flat.

Marta went a few meters across the road's scorching surface, then, as she wasn't a fan of the sound of her soles sticking to the asphalt, made her way forward on the banks. She continued this way past half a kilometer of shacks. The colony seemed to be uninhabited. An electric wire stretched from the other side of the gully to keep cows from escaping, but Marta knew that there wasn't any electricity running through it now, and there hadn't been any herd to corral in the area for years.

The young woman pressed on toward a cottage with a lacquered, khaki-green roof, and she stopped on the doorstep. The door was thick plywood and, above the opening hours, which covered the entirety of the day apart from a break between eight and nine in the morning, an inscription had recently been touched up with red paint, but even so she couldn't quite decide whether it said "RECY-CLE" or "RECOVER." Marta knocked to the right of the inscription.

As in a not terribly funny fairy tale, three old women appeared together before Marta and, without a word, ushered her in. They wore oversized military jackets with torn collars, one of them wearing hers over a blue-flowered farm wife's dress, another around overalls frayed at the knees, and the last over a heap of brown rags so shapeless as to be indefinable. Their heads were furrowed and weathered, but they didn't seem to be in an organic state of disrepair so much as embodying a deplorable state of society. No hunch in their backs, no hooks in their noses or contortions in their hands that might hark back to those witches of the Brothers Grimm fairy tales, but they still gave the impression of being wardens of some alternate reality rather than a camp. Between their lips, for all three of them, in almost exactly the same spot, a string of drool lingered and gleamed.

— Have a seat, said the one in brown rags, the stoutest one, who was almost bald apart from a lock of white hair falling across her left ear.

The others hardly had more hair, but they seemed to have more of a coiffure. The one in the dress had the sort of slim round glasses that shortsighted people always wore; it anchored a stingy wig that was more yellowish than gray.

— Come along now, Marta, have a seat, she said.

Marta settled on a wooden bench, set her bag by her feet, and leaned against the wall. The plaster against her shoulder blades immediately spread coolness through her body.

The wardens took their places throughout the room. All signs pointed to them preparing to carry out an interrogation. Their surly faces, the remnants of brows that they furrowed. Brown Rags, with the lock of hair over her ear, sat behind a small wooden table that clearly served as a desk. Along with the old woman's hands, two notebooks with black covers and a seal and two ballpoints rested on top. Farm Wife's Dress slumped into an imitation leather armchair and betrayed no shame in her legs being splayed apart, much less in her panties, which reproduced a design approved for homesteading women a century earlier, being visible to Marta. The third one, in the overalls that had been mended in the knees twenty times and torn in the knees twenty-one times over the past decade, had just perched atop a stool twenty meters away from Marta. She stank like cabbage soup, nettle gratin, frying oil. She was the first to speak.

— So you've gotten yourself knocked up, she said by way of introduction.

— I was on a mission, Marta protested. I had to blend in with the local population.

Lock over Her Ear guffawed.

— Well, she's blended in, I declare! She's come a right cropper.

Marta bit her lip in a grimace she didn't even try to tamp down.

— It's no laughing matter for me, she said. But it sure seems to be for you three.

The three old women traded looks as they consulted. Marta took the chance to ask for a drink. Overalls got up, went to move around some dishes in the next room, which seemed quite dark, and then came back with a pot full of tea, which she passed around, beginning with Marta. The tea was cold and smelled like vegetable broth. Marta nodded in thanks, then waited for everyone to quench their thirst and Lock over Her Ear to set the pot on the table, straddling the pens and notebooks, as if the bureaucratic materials were wholly useless objects.

— I'm twenty-seven or twenty-eight weeks along, Marta said.

— Don't count on us to be your midwives, Farm Wife's Dress said.

— We didn't ask you to bring us *that*, said Cabbage-Soup Stink.

— Well, that's not the only thing I brought, Marta shot back.

— Go on, Lock over Her Ear said.

— Well, where should I start?

— How about your first impressions? Cabbage-Soup Stink suggested. What was it like back there at first? Was it the way the monks said it would be? Black, floating, silent, angry deities all around? No up or down or tomorrow or yesterday?

Marta shrugged.

— The monks are wrong about all of it, she said. Every bit of it. Their books are just one big fat joke. You go through death and you're in the hereafter, but "hereafter" and "here" aren't the same thing at all. It takes a good bit of time to see what the difference is.

— So there *are* differences? Farm Wife's Dress asked, spreading her mummified legs a bit further apart so Marta could see that, under her homesteading woman's panties, she'd shoved in adult diapers.

— Of course, Marta said, without any further elaboration.

The three interrogators let a fifth of a minute go past, then Lock over Her Ear decided to sum up the situation.

— Marta Bogumil, she said in a tone that in no way disguised its malice. We sent you on a mission so you would tell us what there was beyond the colony. You've been gone ten months without sending back any news. You come back without any sort of heads-up, and a bun in the oven. You've gone and gotten yourself dicked down by some bigmouth out there, is there anything else you've actually done worth telling us about?

Marta sighed. She knew the small talk was over and the actual interrogation was now underway. The old hags were going to bombard her with questions and requests for more detail and further specification and all sorts of criticisms for hours on end, all afternoon, and then all night, without giving her a break or anything to drink.

Maybe because she had some childish hope of buying herself some time, or of unnerving them enough to stop them from holding her feet to the fire and making her look a fool, she got down without telling them what she was about to do, untied the straps of her backpack, and, having opened it, pulled out

23. Theater 2

LYUBA AKUNYAN WAS PERFORMING onstage with a rag doll that was more than half charred. It was a thoroughly mediocre one-act play where she was playing the role of a magician responsible for humanity's disappearance, and before her was a rag-and-bone man who was trying to fix the damage and suggesting a plan for recovering the residue by which she might perhaps be able to revive this vanished species. I was the one told to wear an unfortunately dust-mite-ridden beggar costume and, from the first lines, I'd started suffering unbearable bouts of itchiness. Excited by the gleam of the single bulb warming the tops of our heads and serving as a spotlight, the dust mites were crawling relentlessly every which way all over my skin, most insistently between my thighs and across my back. I was fighting this widespread itching by writhing as discreetly as I could in my chair. Lyuba pretended not to notice my physical distress and shook this lost humanity, this bundle of blackened cloths that, too, had to be throwing yet more little clouds of parasites all over me. We were quite close together and, for some fifteen minutes, we'd been conversing about what was irreversible, about making something out of refuse, about ruined planets and ruling species that had been wiped out. It was a particularly stupid post-exotic fantasy that we had no interest in performing but that the birds had insisted on seeing, threatening to shutter the theater if we didn't comply. The theater was nothing more than a tiny barracks, but, artistic considerations aside, it was the only place still standing amid the dark disaster all around us. So we'd been rehearsing this heavy-going text for a week, and tonight was the premiere.

Personally, I'd been wondering for days whether continuing my work as an actor was worth it when everything outside had been destroyed and our audience would now be solely strange urubus and cormorants, huge puffins, or even worse. I pondered it, but, out of exhaustion, and, I don't feel any shame in saying so, out of violent attachment to Lyuba, I let the matter stand. No doubt the idea of leaving had to be set against the concrete reality that, once I'd stepped out of this house where both our lives—or what stood in for them—had been miraculously preserved, all that would remain would be shapeless, caramelized, dark masses, and there would be nothing to strive for. Nothing existed now, apart from a perpetually twilit, smoky countryside, dusty roads where every passerby sank down to the waist, unbreathable air, indescribable rubble under a sky that never changed, would never change, a moonless, starless, sunless sky. The birds seemed to relish it, they lived in nightmares as if that was normalcy, but I knew perfectly well, we, Lyuba and I, knew perfectly well, that once we'd ventured out there we wouldn't last more than a few hours.

Lyuba stopped herself in the middle of a line and let the silence stretch out, set the doll in her lap, draped her left arm along the chair, and slumped down slightly. We hadn't rehearsed this part of the performance and at first I thought she was improvising, and, in order to keep up the shtick with her, I got out of my seat and tried out a bit of tomfoolery. It was a good way for me to go ahead and scratch away between my legs like some sort of obscene clown. I had no intention of trying to act well, given how odd and badly written this fantasy had been. On the other hand, I was frustrated by the audience's presence. The onlookers were sitting not a meter away from the hallowed performance space; it was an ongoing effort to forget them, since the bulb lit them up almost as much as it did us, as if the playwright had meant to make them silent participants in the performance. Three urubus, all decked out in the same way, oddly dressed like political investigators, their hands in their terribly long khaki ponchos, their immense, inexpressive, golden eyes set deep in their sad faces, huge tufts of brown feathers scattered across speckled, dark pink, sometimes flabby skin. They sat on a bench, almost right by us, and thus far they hadn't moved.

After a few seconds the silence seemed to weigh on us. I walked up to Lyuba, stood behind her, wrapped my arms around her, and, in such a way that the scavengers wouldn't notice, I whispered the rest of her lines. My lips were a hairsbreadth away from the curve of her left cheek and it suddenly seemed icy, reeking terribly like moldering earth and beets. At that moment, Lyuba started to slip inexorably down her chair. She had let go of the doll, she was coming apart, she was slipping. I did my best to hold her by the top of her magician's outfit, but it only took her a few seconds to end up on the floorboards between our two chairs, in a thoroughly untheatrical position like a murdered mammal.

There was no denying the facts: Lyuba had either just passed out or just died. I immediately got down with her. Lyuba wasn't merely my partner, she was my comrade in disaster with whom I'd traversed the apocalypse, and then confronted the aloneness and horror of what had come after. She wasn't breathing. Her body still exuded some warmth, but whiffs of lifelessness, degradation, and the end were already emanating.

I was crouching. I turned toward the audience and made the announcement. The performance had been interrupted for reasons outside the cast's control, viewers were asked to leave the space, all tickets would be reimbursed the following day upon presentation of receipts.

For half a minute, there was nothing, then a whisper grew across the seats. One of the urubus got up. As I was close to the ground, it seemed gigantic. It had a badge on its belly. Its name was Moyom Zachs.

— That's not how it works, it said. You can't just get out of this like that. Its voice was croaky and spiteful.

121

— It's over, I said. The lead actress is dead.

Once again, silence hung over us all, then, once again, a whisper rose up among the birds.

— Death's never been an excuse, Moyom Zachs said. It's up to the audience whether it's over or not.

This absurdity slipped in somewhere beyond my immediate consciousness; I didn't grant it any importance as I set to hugging Lyuba as tight as I could. I was sobbing tearlessly. I was shaken by spasms, but no tears came. Lyuba had been beside me for twelve years of wandering before the apocalypse, and, in the wake of the world's transformation into black space, she had gone on showering the warmth of her affection upon me. Between her and me, she was the more optimistic one, if that word still carried any meaning. There were only the two of us, but our small number didn't keep our metaphysical approaches from diverging. In my eyes, there was no hope whatsoever, and in hers, in my wonderful Lyuba's eyes, there was no such definitiveness when it came to questions beyond our ken. And sometimes she dreamed out loud about a radiant future, say, seven or eight millennia from now, the time it would take for the shadows to pull back and the handful of survivors to rally, to perk up, to rebuild something.

— Okay, the magician's not talking, Moyom Zachs said after letting me cry for half a minute. But the rag-and-bones man can keep going. He'll talk and he'll keep going.

— He has no choice, the second urubu said.

— He can keep going, or he can leave, said the third.

I vaguely recalled that our existence hung by a thread, and that the birds could cut this thread at any moment. Come to think of it, they were now our masters, I mean our absolute masters, our life and death were in their hands. That was one of the consequences of the apocalypse, in any case for Lyuba and me. I didn't try to recall the conditions of the contract that bound us, there was something rather dreamlike and rather sinister about them that I'd pushed deep down in my memories.

I got up, it looked like the birds thought I would step back into the rag-and-bone man's role. I crossed the circle outlined by the bulb and I wanted to slap the second urubu, then I started fighting with the third one, but I wasn't up to it. My close-combat experience went back some decades, and, ever since the apocalypse, I'd lost most of my muscle mass. Moyom Zachs jumped on me, held down my arms, and wrestled me to the ground.

— What's with him? the bird I hadn't even managed to land a blow on asked.

— The last one, the last of the last, Moyom Zachs said.

— Let's throw him out, the third one said.

— Leave me be, I whimpered. It's over. I'll get out. I'll take Lyuba with me and I'll get out.

They conferred. Moyom Zachs was still leaning over me and pinning me down.

— All right, it concluded as it relieved the pressure on my shoulder blades. Go on.

I made my way over to Lyuba, who was just under a meter away, then I stood back up. Moyom Zachs had wrecked my right elbow, but I was still able to move my arms, and, besides, I didn't care about pain and I didn't care about being crippled. I didn't care about any of it. I started pulling Lyuba toward the door.

— Never seen such a badly done play, the second one said, no doubt to humiliate me one last time before I

24. Korchigan

JUST AS THE ENGINE OF HIS LITTLE BOAT exploded, unleashing a shocking amount of gas on fire, Remulus Korchigan miraculously had enough time to see, a hundred meters off, his house tinged by the setting sun and, in a window, the outline of his wife looking toward the landing. His house was in that hoity-toity neoclassical style the nouveaux riches were so fond of. His wife looked like a shapeless mass that he had come to detest over the years. As for his boat motor, it had exploded as soon as he'd touched it, and it was rather unlikely that it had done so for mechanical or natural reasons. This deceptive cliché of happiness—the few steps of a private landing, the gently sloping lawn, the lavish villa, and, behind a slightly parted net curtain, a perfect image of marriage—lasted two or three microseconds, then everything blurred together in a dreadfully yellow surge and Remulus Korchigan, without any conscious thought, driven by the bomb's searing blast, leapt into the water.

There was no current in this spot and the boat had barely drifted from the side of the pontoon. He wasn't much of a swimmer, but Korchigan was quite capable of reaching the bank's stone wall or the pontoon with a few breaststrokes. But the situation was worsening quickly, as a puddle of fire cut him off and, while he was swimming away, he saw that the gas had spread across a good part of the swath he had to cross to reach solid ground. He headed toward the boat, touched the hull, then lost heart. He couldn't get a proper hold, and he knew he didn't have the strength or the flexibility to climb aboard, and, in any case, blazing streaks of red were twisting up above and making it clear that it wasn't wise to seek shelter there. He turned around and immediately panicked. His clothes and shoes were weighing him down; he was barely able to keep his head dry. The water was right at his lips. He had an image in his head of the river down below, which in this spot was deep and silty, and he paddled in place, then he decided that he'd have to get back to shore, no matter the cost, and do his best not to get caught in the current. At the bottom of the lawn, the walls plunged straight into the water and, on the other side of the pontoon, everyone could see how strong the current was that would push a small boat out to the nearest lake. Remulus Korchigan slapped and pounded and splashed the water around him in a long string of irrational gestures, and suddenly he felt like he'd lost all his bearings, or at least most of them, because this boundary of stinking fire was still right by him, up close, and he absolutely had to escape it. He could smell the fuel in the water that he spat out, he could feel the heat mounting, and he could see the flames splitting up in new floating layers all around him and growing more and more threatening. Because of these orange braids, the small landing had become inaccessible. Once the stench was too stifling and too hot, he stopped splashing around, saw between two yellow eddies the sky high above, the not-too-mossy wall nearby, and, farther off, the top floor of the faux-Ionic colonnade with its white roof. Then he decided to dive.

He was fifty-six years old, didn't care much for sports, and had a rather unambiguous aversion to swimming, but, considering that he had to save his skin, he took a deep breath and descended. Before his eyes, at breakneck speed, flashed numerous action-film underwater sequences, which he consolidated at even greater speed and decided to reproduce as best as he could, as fast as he could. When he was sitting in his living room, he was in the habit of holding his breath as he accompanied heroes and heroines in their determined attempts to forge forward in a hostile, watery realm, staying well ahead of carnivorous fish or even aliens, or wresting open car doors, surrounded by shadows and seaweed, or continuing a knife fight that had begun on solid ground. He didn't move in his chair, but even so he still wasn't able to hold his breath for as long as those extraordinary athletes and righters of wrongs of the small screen did. And yet those film images would bolster his courage and even inspire him for those first four or five seconds, they would be vivid in his mind, buttressing his consciousness and showing him what best to do beneath the surface. That was why the first seconds unfurled so well. The water hadn't yet snaked its way into his sinuses, his breaststrokes were already pulling him away from the most worrisome orange gleams, and his eyes, which he'd never in all his life been able to open underwater, bore this contact with the blurry water mostly unbothered. And so he traversed several paltry meters without feeling an urgent need to renew the air that had filled his lungs, then his feet, weighed down by shoes, dragged downward, his calves rubbed against some vile vegetation, he felt like a bit of the river's silt had made it past his lips, and he panicked. The fear of drowning darkened his thoughts, a spasm ran through his stomach that he immediately took for a prelude to the water's fatal inrush down his windpipe. Overcome by a reflexive dance, without the least bit of coordination between his upper and lower limbs, he abandoned any pretense, clumsily spat out his oxygen reserves, and resurfaced, gasping, wheezing, thrashing. The puddle of fire had spread out two meters away, delineating a narrow corridor toward the rundown skeleton of the former jetty. The new jetty's pontoon was barely visible through a veil of black smoke. The boat hadn't been pulled away by the current and wavered, half-ablaze, as if it were determined to stay put, no matter what, where it was most often moored, as if proving its idiotic, animal loyalty.

Remulus Korchigan didn't call for help and didn't signal where he was. He wasn't paranoid, but, from the outset, he'd known that this was no accident. He'd heard an explosion that couldn't be explained away by mechanical causes. An engine misfire couldn't spark such a swift, brutal inferno; there had to be some sort of hellish setup in this matter. My daughter, he thought. Tamara Korchigan. My daughter and my son-in-law Ulgang Schnatz. He didn't have any time to follow this train of thought, but, as he felt his legs drifting downward again, and as the gap in the fire might close at any moment, he pushed away his thoughts and advanced between the flames toward the old jetty. There were only remnants of rotting piles and planks, and briars prevented all from getting to the land adjoining the villa. As he knew that he was evading, at least momentarily, an assassination attempt, he did his best to hide among the ruins. He stayed down in the mud, his head up above, his feet touching the lake's bottom. He tried to move as little as possible. I'll just stay here a minute, he thought. We'll see what happens.

Jimmy Korchigan, his eighteen-year-old son, had just come out on the pontoon. He held a pole with a hook at its end and, seemingly unbothered by the thick fumes and rumblings that wafted his way, he started prodding among the oily wavelets splashing or bubbling beneath his feet. His actions evinced nonchalance. He dragged his gaff toward the edge of the flames almost aimlessly, as if for the fun of it. Not long after, he was joined by his mother, Lolla Korchigan, who seemed to be more furious than worried. From his hiding spot, Remulus Korchigan didn't miss a syllable of their conversation, since silence hung over the river and the son and his mother weren't bothering to whisper.

— He's nowhere to be found, said Jimmy Korchigan.

— Go deeper, Lolla Korchigan said. Maybe he's floating further down.

— Or he was carried away by the current, the son replied.

— What if he's still in the boat?

— You said you saw him fall overboard.

— I'm not so sure about that.

The two of them were gesticulating in the black haze dotted by orange flames, and it was a somewhat stunning scene: mother and son, arguing with each other rather than joining forces to find the body of Remulus Korchigan. Jimmy was nearly two meters tall, a slender, twitching thing, while Lolla Korchigan looked just like a small fat hen. A comical pairing, Remulus Korchigan found himself thinking, as he huddled in the old jetty's darkness. The back of his head was pressed against a tuft of those questionable plants that bloomed in the worst corners of cobblestones, between crumbling planks and spiderwebs, far from light and all too close to the murky water.

Just hang in there, Remulus Korchigan, he thought, not moving his head, doing his best to tamp down his deep-seated fear of creepy-crawlies and spiders. It's just plants, and a bit of rubbish. Not like your family members.

— Try deeper, Lolla Korchigan said.

— No point, Jimmy Korchigan replied.

— I'll be the judge of that. Give it here.

Mother and son were now bickering about the spear. Thank goodness there's no way they can get to the old jetty, Remulus Korchigan thought. If I don't move, if I go unnoticed, they won't think to look for me here.

The ruined boat drew closer to the river. As most of the fuel flames were sputtering out, it would crash against the wall on the other side of the pontoon.

Ulgang Schnatz, the son-in-law, had just appeared at the top of the lawn. He ambled down the slope and

25. Myriamne Shuygo

THE REFUGEE CAMP was eight kilometers away from the city, or rather, from everyone in general. Anybody going there had to stop at three successive checkpoints, the third and last being a long dark tunnel in which the traveler had to hold his or her breath for at least three minutes, and move as fast as possible. Only at the other end of the airlock could spasmodic lungs be calmed and eyes opened to a blazing sun. Anyone who dared to make this trip would immediately be assaulted by the violence that was the desert and the fecal odors all around. They were most often greeted by four or five goons from the local mafia purportedly in charge of security. The mafias might change, but their representatives' demands were always the same, ten dollars and half the medicine you had on you, a blow job, and one finger if you'd come without anything.

For months, the camp had been full to bursting. Then it had been gradually emptied out due to several things: supply-chain challenges, catastrophic sanitary conditions, cholera epidemics, the all-powerful wind, and the atrocities the child soldiers had carried out. Those disasters were compounded by the city-dwellers' utter lack of compassion. The good people's hostility was unremitting and underscored by the two horrific incursions that pogromists had made, which they called "the Indian ambush" and which had left hundreds wounded and dead.

The Organization had assigned me, along with Eliana Valoustani, to sneak into the camp, to draw up an accurate list of traffickers, bandits, and those collaborating or having collaborated with the pogromists, then, once the list of targets was finalized and sent to the Action headquarters, to undertake two or three assassinations before sneaking out and passing the baton to experts like Abimaël Fischmann or Bordushvili, who would have done the dirty work before the words were out of our mouths.

Eliana Valoustani stood beside me in front of the small "screening" group. There were five of them, all in grotesque military outfits and wearing filthy wigs that were in fact just recently flensed scalps. They weren't teenagers anymore, but they looked like child soldiers, their eyes gleaming as if drugged. We caught our breath after crossing the access tunnel and we could feel the sun baking our faces, our ears, our hands. The air reeked with the dust and the pit latrines. We'd opted to enter the camp as medical personnel and our bags were heavy with an astonishing quantity of medicine, mostly pain-killers, antibiotics, antidiarrheals, and sterilizing equipment. The youngsters listened to us and made lewd, disturbing jokes as they poked around in our luggage and pulled out all the bottles of 180-proof alcohol, clearly intent on drinking it. They got in our faces and, while rummaging through our haversacks, they fondled us or jostled us. They let out loud, filthy sighs. Their disgusting jackets bore streaks of blood, their ears and cheeks were caked with brown crusts. We finally breathed freely when one of the two older ones, his forehead squeezed under a scalp with long, greasy, black hair, urged us to follow him on pretext of "additional identification." He had to be the leader. He was holding our passes in his filthy hands and hadn't bothered to look at them. His buddies snickered like idiots.

The camp covered both flanks of a gently sloping valley, which we could see from the top of the last checkpoint. The tents had originally been set in a geometric layout, but, once the humanitarian missions had left, it hadn't taken long for that plan to go to pieces, and the pattern turned nightmarish, the earliest tents being enlarged with mongrel structures, made out of the remnants of a previous slum and debris stolen from the outskirts. There was no logic anymore to the various paths or to the overarching geography of what had become a sprawling home for vagrants. The big blue hospital tent had been half burned down by pogromists and, in any case, the medical devices had been rendered inoperable or sold off to questionable city clinics. The mafias oversaw everything with absolute cruelty and terrifying fickleness, and yet they had somehow imposed a semblance of order that kept people from settling scores and turning anarchic.

As we hadn't hurried to follow this unsavory man, he turned and addressed me. He knew how to read, he'd retained the name on my papers:

— Myriamne Shuygo, can you tell me what the difference is between you and your friend?

Eliana Valoustani and I glanced at one another.

— She's a doctor, and so am I, I said. There's no difference between us.

— Oh yes, there's a difference, the gang leader said. She's pretty and you're ugly as sin.

The others burst out laughing. They were slapping their thighs, their mouths wide open as they gasped and let out horrid guffaws.

My physical appearance didn't matter to me. Twenty years ago, while hunting Ybürs, I'd been snared by two members of the Werschwell Faction. For some unclear reason, maybe because they'd already met their quota of murders, and because they'd been drunk enough, they simply slashed my face and let me go. I'd led a normal life after that in the Party schools and I hadn't really suffered from those wounds. Beauty, ugliness, and handicap didn't matter in the Organization; what counted was intellectual and martial competence, and moral integrity. But it's true that Eliana Valoustani didn't have the swollen, pallid cross that I did on my left cheek, stretching up to my forehead. In that aspect, she was clearly different.

Once the laughter had subsided, the atmosphere was even more fraught. It was evident that they wouldn't simply requisition our ethyl alcohol, that they would need something more from us. We'd trained for this mission and for this "screening" and we'd learned how to endure rape, gang rape, and blow jobs in the context of wool grease, stenches, and sickness. We'd acquainted ourselves with horror and sacrifice, but with the intent of avoiding horror and sacrifice as much as possible.

— Myriamne Shuygo, you can take your belongings and head to the camp hospital, Long Greasy Black Hair said, waving his hand toward some unclear part of the camp.

I looked at the deplorable labyrinth of the valley floor. Beside the ruins of the huge blue tent, there were sticks covered by blue canvas. Maybe that was what he meant by hospital.

— Eliana Valoustani will be staying here, the gang leader said. We have to verify some details.

Eliana Valoustani turned toward me. She was a dozen meters away. I could see panic in her eyes. She didn't show it, she stood upright and didn't waver, her face was impassive, but I knew her well enough to see something in her that was quickly coming apart. We understood this phenomenon, a simultaneously rational and irrational phenomenon, a brutal, uncontrollable inability to stab the monster in the heart, an inner breakdown that no process could prevent, least of all when it mattered most. It was a weakness that no amount of training could do away with. We called it "level-one amok," and we knew that it could happen to anyone, to women and men alike, without any warning, just like death. Deep in Eliana Valoustani's gaze, that glimmer was all too legible: that was level-one amok, and she wasn't going to let herself undergo the ordeal that awaited her if she obeyed the gang leader.

I suspected that we might be able to remedy the situation by standing firm.

— We've already given you half the medicines, I said sharply. The verification's done. Give us our papers and leave us alone.

Long Greasy Black Hair paused and, for a second, I thought he might comply. We were doctors, after all, and that vested us with an almost magical authority. I underscored this in walking over to our bags to close them, pull them on, and help Eliana Valoustani do so as well, thereby putting an end to the discussion. Whether or not we got our passes back hardly mattered.

As I started to buckle my bag across my body, Long Greasy Black Hair suddenly got angry and grabbed Eliana Valoustani by the shoulder, and it was clear he wanted to drag her into one of those filthy "screening" tents. I heard Eliana Valoustani let out an angry yell and immediately, contrary to how we had been taught to handle this sort of scene, go ballistic on her aggressor. The arm that had grabbed her immediately snapped in two, the man didn't have time to cry out, and a perfectly aimed forearm blow had already broken the cartilage of his trachea. As a demonstration of martial skills, I admired the artistry in Eliana Valoustani's actions, and then, in the same breath, I realized that our entry into the camp was going off the rails, that it had turned into a nightmare sequence and our mission was henceforth doomed to failure. Eliana Valoustani had finished the guy off with a backward kick that shattered his forehead and, presumably, everything behind it. Then she pulled herself back together, striking an impeccable, well-balanced figure, almost smiling as she had overcome her fear, was now herself again after this level-one amok moment, and she growled to all the present company:

— Are there any other verifications to be taken care of?

The others were stunned, petrified. Their eyes swiveled from their leader's corpse, its disgusting wig having slipped off to reveal a shattered skull glistening with sebum, to

26. Soldatov

ALTHOUGH HE HADN'T BEEN INVITED, Soldatov slipped into the receiving line of Sasha Yomoshiguin's distant relatives and sanctimonious attendees, and once he'd reached both the table at its end and one of Yomoshiguin's sisters-in-law, Leila Yomoshiguina, he set down an offering envelope in gray ink. His eyes met her black, questioning ones, wet and gleaming exactly like those he had glimpsed four days earlier, when she was stuck in the car's backseat, awaiting a death that hadn't come. He didn't blink, but he felt something tugging at the bottom of his throat. He hadn't been prepared to see her here and he wondered if she had recognized him. Stifling his impulse to swallow, he calmly recited the amount the envelope contained. The woman looked down and made a small apologetic curtsy. She asked him to repeat himself. She hadn't heard right, or she wasn't sure she'd heard right, and she didn't want to write an incorrect number down in the registry. There was a momentary, interminable confusion in which she stared intently at the envelope, unable to decipher the scrawl that Soldatov had made illegible with the sorts of fantastical embellishments that half-illiterates draw when told to sign official documents. "Thirty dollars," Soldatov repeated in a muffled tone, as if confiding something. It was a reasonable amount, somewhat stingy, but a typical contribution for someone outside the family who wanted to take part in the wake, offer condolences, and burn some incense before the portrait of the dearly departed. Leila looked up at Soldatov again. In this obsidian gleam Soldatov saw indifference rather than contempt. "She doesn't recognize me," he thought before genuflecting respectfully, then he stepped aside for the next visitor.

Soldatov, in any case, wasn't terribly recognizable. He'd shaved his head, knotted a black tie around his neck, and was wearing a standard outfit, a charcoal-gray suit that left him anonymous amid so many nearly identical men here for Yomoshiguin's wake. On the belt concealed by his jacket he wore the gun with which, four days earlier, he'd shot Sasha Yomoshiguin and his driver.

He slowly made his way toward the altar. Behind it was a huge photograph of Sasha Yomoshiguin, two corners of which were covered with a black ribbon. The man whose portrait now faced Soldatov barely resembled the one he'd left two bullets in, and who, in the car, had looked like a drunken cow, lewdly entangled with his sister-in-law, lewdly groping his sister-in-law Leila's bosom. At the moment he opened fire, Soldatov had already realized that he was executing the notorious Yomoshiguin, the brother of the man he'd been told to kill, but he hadn't wavered, partly because the driver and bodyguard had already been incapacitated, and there was no taking half-measures at that point, partly because his personal ethics condemned adultery and he deemed this situation offensive. During the fraction of a second in which he'd decided to fire a second bullet into Yomoshiguin's head, this aspect of an honor killing had been added to the simple assassination, as if, deep down, he was correcting his targeting error and avenging the sullied reputation of Boris Yomoshiguin, the husband Leila Yomoshiguina was currently betraying. That was when he met the adulterous woman's gaze, a magnificent gaze that fear had widened and that, contrary to all the principles underlying a well-run operation, which required the elimination of any witnesses, had convinced him not to send her the same way her lover and her driver had already gone. "Too bad," he thought. "I'll take care of her along with Boris Yomoshiguin, at Sasha's wake."

He made his way to the altar, bowed down, lit a stick of incense that he then set in a bowl among the ashes of dozens and hundreds of others, bowed a second time. He did so while focusing on his actions so as not to attract attention through any misstep that would have, even in a small way, violated the ritual. He also tried not to focus too much on the extremely dangerous situation in which he found himself, as he had turned his back on the crowd, and, most especially, Boris Yomoshiguin's bodyguards, whom he could tell were close by, not even ten meters away. He bowed a third time. "Even if it's highly unlikely that they'd aim and shoot at the altar, they could still mow me down," he thought. "If they notice an odd lump on my belt, they'll be on alert and, as soon as I've turned around, they'll neutralize me, by gunfire or by some other way."

The air reeked of incense sticks and spirals burning up. On Soldatov's left, a priest in a white habit, with a long mourning cap, was reciting incomprehensible prayers and intonations. "Maybe these are the last impressions of the world that I'm receiving," he thought, "the final images before they riddle me with bullets, the final sounds, the final smells that will be imprinted in my memory before my brain gives out."

Unhurriedly, savoring each and every sensation like a condemned man, he turned around. As if nothing odd were happening in the room, he let out the oxygen he had been holding in and stopped again. "Well, not right now, I guess," he thought. To his left he could see the compact, well-dressed, but still unnerving mass of fellows surrounding Boris Yomoshiguin who, in a way, were shielding him from the rest of the mourners. For safety reasons, Yomoshiguin wasn't sitting where the family hierarchy ought to have put him, at the far end of the first tier; it would have made him too easy a target. Soldatov genuflected before the group, not looking up, thereby presenting his condolences to an undifferentiated mass, then he went back to the group of the distant most members of the family. All the people there were affecting the usual contemplative look, straight backs, stiff necks, blank stares, unthinking and almost unblinking.

Among those attending the ceremony was, most likely, his client, the one who had paid Soldatov to off Yomoshiguin, not just any Yomoshiguin, but Boris Yomoshiguin and nobody else, and who must be livid that he was going to the cremation of Sasha Yomoshiguin rather than that of his brother. Once Soldatov was sitting well away from the crowd, he ran his eyes over the heads present, looking away several times so as not to attract attention. Apart from the bodyguards, he saw three people who showed small indications of impatience, two men and a woman. "As far as methods go, that's not much use, " he thought. "It's meaningless." One of the men was in the family's third tier, every so often he shifted his hands. The other man was standing among the officials. He sometimes looked over to scrutinize Yomoshiguin and his goons, then he started feigning contemplativeness. And the woman was on her feet between the table where Leila Yomoshiguina held sway and some four monks who seemed to be presiding over an ancillary or perhaps unrelated ceremony. She, like Leila Yomoshiguina, was in mourning clothes, her hair held in place with a hood-shaped square of linen, but, rather than exuding absolute serenity, she seemed somewhat nervous. She had to be the widow, but nobody seemed interested in accompanying her to the altar or making an appearance at her side. "It's meaningless," Soldatov kept thinking. "And maybe the client has that much self-control. It could be anyone in this room, if it's even someone here at all."

A second priest and his acolytes had come to lend the first one a helping hand, and now, in the silence, new prayers set to the tempo of new drumbeats rang out solidly. The homages continued: visitors came one after another to the altar, breaking apart, then turning their backs to the dearly departed's photograph while solemnly hailing the assemblage. Soldatov mulled over how the ceremony didn't quite match up to what he'd experienced in religious contexts. The fundamentals were being respected, yes, but the ritual was, in his opinion, veering somewhat off course. The next-of-kin weren't surrounding the widow; several women in the family didn't have their heads covered; the monks were following atypical practices, as if they belonged to a rival sect that had just made an eleventh-hour, badly negotiated alliance; the bodyguards were sitting in a pew that should have been reserved for a part of the family by marriage, or for dignitaries. As for those who were paying homage to the dead man, they weren't listening to the priest's injunctions, but repeating the gestures they'd been taught elsewhere, some of them crushing the ashes between their thumb and forefinger before setting their incense stick in the bowl, others abstained, some only bowed once before the portrait of Yomoshiguin, others had, like Soldatov, bowed three times. "There's no respect anymore," Soldatov thought. "Religion is just going to the dogs. Even the officiants aren't being sticklers anymore."

Soldatov, in fact, wasn't all that keen to put a face to the client who had ordered the assassination, no more than he was in dissecting these variations on funerary rites. He was just waiting for an opportune moment to act. Once the coffin was in the crematorium's antechamber, the family would come together and walk slowly past the rows of those not in the family and those who were distant relatives. Boris Yomoshiguin would lead them all before sitting up in front of his brother's body. Soldatov would then be in the perfect position to fell him, to shoot up the bodyguards, and disappear through a side door. Then, if all went well, he'd reach the agreed-upon meeting place and receive the second, bigger tranche of his fee. The side door that ensured his escape was less than ten meters away from where he now stood. He had made sure the night before that it was never locked, and led to a tunnel that would allow him to vanish in a matter of seconds, according to an itinerary that

27. Skvortsov

At the start of the week, Ogul Skvortsov passed away offhand-edly, and, that Saturday, the Borbodjian brothers came into the old timber house and started shaking drums, tinkling bells, trudging around walls, and growling their appeals to the Five Black Heavens, the Three Snouts, the Great Leaders. They seemed stricken by madness rather than endowed with any shamanistic knowledge. They reeked sweat, vodka, and smoke; tin amulets and bells jangled from the hems of their coats; the planks shaken by their comings and goings released dusty clouds.

Ogul Skvortsov climbed out of the chair he'd been ensconced in, unmoving, for the preceding days and nights. He grabbed a broom, opened the door, and shoved the brothers outside. "I'm not one of yours!" he declared. The brothers apologized, bowed respectfully, and went back home. They lived nearby, on the next street over, and there, in a filthy isba, they'd opened a shamanic apothecary: assistance was advertised for wandering through black spaces, connections with the Seven Black Heavens, connections & conversations with crows, eagles, corpses, dances with moon-drums, ritual songs, ritual cries & shrieks, reassurances for the dying, quests for animals or vanished beloveds, &c. Their business didn't really adhere to legal accounting requirements and certainly didn't follow hygiene and safety regulations, and so various administrative officials barged right into the hovel, wielding cease-and-desist orders as well as sternly worded letters, but the brothers never bestirred themselves from their bedsteads and simply gave vague replies, pretending not to understand a whit of their bureaucratese and, more broadly, any human tongue. It had to be said the stifling room they lived in was sunken in terrible darkness, not to mention rotting meat, potatoes, sleep, and farts; a chaotic atmosphere befitting another world reigned, such that the functionaries didn't stay long before slinking away and disappearing.

Ogul Skvortsov had been a taciturn man all his life, and after his death this characteristic had only deepened, but the Borbodjian brothers incident now allowed him to acquaint himself with his new voice from beyond the grave. It was inelegant, far too hoarse. For the first time in five days he'd heard himself bemoaning the brothers, and the impression that had left upon him had been so horrendous that he'd decided not to utter any further word, not even in the middle of an unsteady lowing. "That's enough," he thought. "It's obscene to speak, in any case." He sat back down and was silent.

For the whole summer, Ogul Skvortsov remained seated in that way, making no further gesture or speaking the least word. He spent his days and his nights meditating on the oddness of existence, the planets' course, the whirlwind worlds, and the cockroaches screeching not far off, gnawing at the last bits of grease and bread.

At the summer's end, the cockroaches that had exhausted all the provisions that might still interest them left the house, and, in the room where Ogul Skvortsov dozed, the sounds of footfalls and chewing abated. Outside, shadows fall over the world little by little, and sometimes during the day passersby drew near and then, for some unknown reason, drew back and hastened their footsteps, or whispered but did not enter, then were off. "What's come over them," Skvortsov wondered, "what are those damned fools so afraid of?"

In mid-October two policemen came in. The same way as the Borbodjian brothers, but without any bells or drums as big as the moon; they went around the walls and poked their noses hither and thither, and for a good few minutes they were wholly unaware of the being seated in the middle of the room. In their wake, the air now smelled like military uniforms, tobacco, and the piss-poor authority the camp wardens or their ilk were vested with. Then they stopped their futile investigations and decided to wrap up their assigned mission. The first one, a young blond guy with a few small scars on his forehead, pulled out his rifle and leaned it against the chair Skvortsov was in. As for the second one, a stern fortysomething with a shaved head, he pulled an official document out of his pocket and read the absurdly, bureaucratically complex sentences without any semblance of fluidity. As far as Skvortsov could tell, it was a cease-and-desist, namely an insistence on leaving immediately with these forces of order. "Where do you think you're taking me?" Skvortsov asked. The fortysomething pursed his lips. "You know exactly where," he said. "A hole."

Skvortsov let three seconds go by, and then he took the rifle and opened fire. "You first," he declared. The reverberation of the blast broke the silence for a long while, the smoke and stench of gunpowder faded away, the blond guy fell backward, and, after a rather vaguely defined stretch of time, found himself belly-up and immobile on the floorboards. "Article 58.9, harmful elements," the shaved head continued as he held the court order. He seemed not to be able to act until he'd finished reading it, maybe out of respect for a well-established legal albeit inane process. "First name Ogul, patronymic unknown, last name Skvortsov, illiterate, residence listed *infra*, nationality unknown, punishment not administered for reasons unknown." On the floor, the first policemen was starting to move his arms around weakly and moan. The reader paused to look at his comrade. For several minutes, the wounded man struggled to crawl toward the door. Once he was a meter away from the threshold, he suddenly stiffened and froze. The fortysomething shifted his attention back to the administrative document and, after running his eyes down it without opening his lips, summarized it in common language. "You gotta be buried," he said. "It's the law."

"You first," Skvortsov groaned. "I'm not one of yours." He opened fire a second time but missed his target. The policeman jumped on him, wrested the rifle out of his hands, then stood in front of him, wheezing and furious. "Scum like you, I oughta . . ." he said, brandishing the gun. His sentence hung, unfinished, and, for a few seconds, it seemed just about to veer toward a conclusion, but nothing more was added, apart from a despairing hiccup. The man shrugged, slung his rifle over his shoulder, opened the door, pulled and dragged the scarred blond guy, who was no longer responsive, outside, and before closing the door and heading to the nearest police headquarters, he pulled the pin out of a grenade and threw it inside Skvortsov's house.

The grenade exploded, resulting in a deafening noise in the enclosed space, but the explosive surge had no effect on Ogul Skvortsov and, five or six days later, all the toxic substances and charred remains had already dissolved into nothingness. It was as if the policemen's incursion hadn't happened.

In the house, silence and calm eventually reigned anew. November came, and with it snowfalls, and winter's immense, traditional lack of noise and movement. At the month's end, Ogul Skvortsov got up and headed to the second room in his place, the bedroom where, some years earlier, he had still slept with his wife, Lidia Schmein, or rather shared with her the insomnia that tortured them both. They had known each other from childhood and they were still together notwithstanding separations and interminable stays in the camps. When they'd finally been able to live together without fear, without any impending prospect of being torn apart or imprisoned, they were already an old couple, and after a cruel twist of fate their happy coexistence hadn't lasted.

Lidia Moyssieyevna had vanished without any warning, and all attempts to locate her had been unsuccessful. Skvortsov suspected she had been arrested as a witness in one matter or another, that she had fallen ill while in custody, and the guards, unsure what to do with her, had probably finished her off and shipped her far away, into the forest, so the wolves could autopsy her and give her the most suitable funerary scattering possible.

He walked up to the mirror hung on the wall between the chest and the nightstand, and he exhaled on it to figure out where he ranked in the biological hierarchy. He was feeling out of sorts, and he wanted some proof, despite everything, of his existence. He didn't harbor many illusions but, when no steam condensed on the glass, he let out an exasperated cry. "Those damned fools," he grumbled, "they had to go and take *that* away from me!"

The following day and night, and the next day, and the day after that, he stayed by the bed he'd shared with his wife, adjusting the pillows every so often, contemplating the emptiness, the rarefied air, the half-darkness, sometimes standing still by the window but not looking outside. He was reflecting. "Lidia Schmein," he repeated for an entire night, barely parting his lips. Then he decided to call the Borbodjian brothers.

"With their filthy crow brothers, black heavens, and great leaders, they'll be able to manage something," he thought.

He went and sat back in the main room. "I'll call them," he thought.

It was icy cold. They had weathered so much over the decades, and yet the house's timbers never stopped cracking, especially in the darkest hours of the night. Almost nobody ever went out anymore in the snow the first week of December. On the side of the street where the Borbodjian brothers lived, someone could be heard clearing a path with a shovel, and as night fell, there was also

28. Grondin

The name Kerrigan, then a rain-blurred word that could have read Recoverer or Recycler, then the line Fring Away Company. Not putting much stock in it, much less understanding what it meant, Grondin fiddled with the soggy business card the guy had thrown at him before disappearing in the gardens by the dark street. Two policemen lay beside him in the rain, surrounded by black puddles that could just as easily have been pooling blood as the natural flow of water from the heavens. The sidewalk crackled beneath the raindrops. As the spurts and splashes buffeted his eyes, Grondin sat up and scanned the vicinity. Night, a thick, empty night. No residential blocks, only the unlit frontage of administrative buildings. Trees, grilles, flooded tar, a mad downpour, no wind. On the other side of the road, a closed-down Pakistani restaurant, its sign illegible, its glass panes protected by wooden shutters, suggesting that the neighborhood wasn't solely the province of ministers or head offices. Apart from the two corpses that up to the previous minute hadn't been, who up until the previous minute had thought that they were on an easy mission, that they were escorting a witness under state protection to their service car, who had been in a rush so as not to get drenched but who in fact had rushed headlong into an encounter with a special-forces Stechkin—apart from these two bodies now splayed across the ground in a jumble of limbs and raincoats, there was no one. The avenue was badly lit, hideously damp, and bathed in a nearly tropical heat. A hundred meters off, far from the streetlights, someone was making a call in a phone booth, or sheltering in it. Grondin got up, uttered a brief prayer for the deceased's trip, and waded somewhat undecidedly toward the booth.

All this had happened in a matter of minutes: the killer had joined them, and once he'd started shooting, the policemen had abruptly thrown Grondin to the ground. They'd then rolled to the side, pulling out their weapons, but they hadn't had any time to counterattack. The killer had finished them off immediately, had crouched down to take their guns, and, without a glance at Grondin, he'd thrown the man a strip of cold card stock, and, in doing so, had disappeared.

The phone booth was occupied by two people. A very young couple was kissing passionately and, even if they didn't quite appear intent on going all the way sexually, they seemed absorbed enough in their embrace to have completely forgotten about the outside world. Condensation had fogged up a good portion of the panes, the darkness barely tempered by a small light, and, in this confined space, they must have felt at home and at ease. Grondin tapped on the dripping glass to signal his presence and hurry their fervent activity along, then he waited a good half-dozen seconds and, as nothing seemed to be changing, he tried opening the door as much as he could, which folded inward and was hindered by the boy's body, then he stuck his hand in the gap and touched one of the two partners, maybe the boy, or perhaps the girl, where the shoulder met the neck. This contact with bare, moist skin under a layer of sweat- and desire-soaked peach fuzz disgusted him. In the booth, the girl let out a shriek. Grondin pulled back his hand. The door banged shut and one of the two youngsters, certainly by accident rather than malice, yanked the cord for the fluorescent light radiating faintly in the compartment. The already-dim lamp went out completely. The girl stopped screaming.

In the dark street the rain cadenced the subsequent instants: the two's stillness, the youngsters' frenetic sighs, Grondin's erratic breathing. The couple had concluded their amorous entanglement. Grondin could feel the water pattering on his shaved skull and slipping down his spine. His jacket was leather and protected him, but there was no way to pull the collar tight. As for his pants, those were soaked. His shoes were sopping wet.

Those kids are terrified of me, he thought.

— Hey, he said loudly. I gotta make a call. Been a bit of a ruckus. Need to get the police here.

Everything stayed silent in the enclosure as Grondin counted to three, then, in a monotone, came the boy's self-satisfied declaration.

— Hey, asswipe, how about scram. Ain't we going nowhere.

Grondin took a step forward, leaned his full weight on the door, slipped his hand in the dark opening, and grabbed a bit of shoulder or belly flab, then he pulled hard on what he'd seized. The boy's head appeared and Grondin dug his fingers deep into that face. The girl started wailing shrilly. The door didn't make it easy for the boy, who instinctively understood that he shouldn't resist and that, on the contrary, the faster he was out of this booth, the sooner he would be freed of this horrific feeling of being pinched to the bone by an iron grip. The only thing the boy was fighting, in fact, was the door impeding his exit. Grondin finally got him all the way out and threw him onto the sidewalk like a shapeless mass, then, after giving him a kick in the temple so he'd go quiet, he let him go and turned to the girl who was still yelling. He pointed the way she should go and stepped back to let her do so. The girl wavered for half a second then she stopped bawling and made herself scarce. Grondin saw her sinking down to the boy, as if to administer first aid, then getting up and doing nothing in particular, maybe because she had no experience as a nurse or maybe because she was too shocked to act. He didn't care about them anymore.

The phone booth door had been damaged and he didn't try to pull it shut behind him to ensure any privacy. He actually wanted to air out the space where, in addition to the usual stench of grime and solidified spittle, the strong odors of bodies on the brink of orgasm lingered. He picked up the handset, dialed the Fring Away Company number. Then he realized that he didn't have the dollar coin he needed to make the connection, and he set the phone back on the hook. He'd have to go back out to scrounge up a dollar from one of the children.

The rain was even fiercer now, meticulously perpendicular to the ground, and oppressive. The boy was groaning, his arms and legs splayed, his eyes shut, his face washed clean, and he seemed to be doing a dead man's float in a shadowy swimming pool. The girl might have tried to whisper something in his ear, but, when

Grondin approached them, she stood up sharply and pulled back while adjusting her blouse or what remained of it.

— Pardon me, said Grondin. Could you kindly lend me a dollar?

As the girl didn't react, he crouched down and reached into the boy's pockets. The right-hand one was filled with money: four coins and two or three already-spongy bills. Grondin took the coins. The girl watched him, sniffling, her hair long and dripping down to her stomach, and she wore a ridiculous pink blouse with far too many buttons missing and black jeans torn at the knees.

Grondin clambered back into the phone booth. The apparatus took his dollar in halfway as he dialed the number on the business card again. On the other end of the line, someone picked up immediately, and the dollar fell all the way in with a loud jangle.

— Hello? came an old woman's voice, which then fell silent.

— Am I speaking to Kerrigan? Grondin asked.

— Hello? the old woman repeated.

Grondin scowled and looked at the scene outside. In the distance, the policemen's corpses were just barely visible. A car had just stopped beside them. Nobody got out. The headlights lit up the street, which had become a river. Slowly, the car maneuvered, made a U-turn, and then drove off. Closer by, the girl and the boy were shifting. The girl was helping the boy to sit up in the gutter, as if he needed to have his butt in even more water than what was already on the sidewalk. The girl wasn't talking, the boy was swaying and stammering a few syllables muddled completely by the rain's roar.

— I was told to call Kerrigan, Grondin enunciated as if he were speaking to a mentally deficient person or a deaf woman. May I please speak with him?

To Grondin's frustration the old woman asked him who was on the line, and that was when the car reappeared and braked in front of the policemen, spraying the two bodies with a sheet of water. No passenger bothered to get out and examine the dead up close. However, the killer, who must have been crouching behind the bushes all this while, came out of his hiding spot and strode across the sidewalk. He sidestepped the inert victims, floundered toward the car, opened the back passenger door, and got in.

At the same moment, the old woman changed her tone.

— Hey, asswipe, how about scram, she said, and hung up.

The car

29. Quantz

THAT MORNING, URAN QUANTZ woke up in a cold sweat, and even though hot, heavy air was rolling across his body from the open window, he was still shivering. His skin was clammy, but not overly so. The trickle of perspiration was part of his dream. He had been dreaming that he'd missed the bus. He'd run after it, in the increasingly wispy dust of the road, and the vehicle was pulling farther and farther away, eventually disappearing behind a rise in the road; it did not reappear again.

Quantz got out of bed and left the hut. It was early, just before dawn. No birds were singing. In the courtyard, there was nobody. The innkeeper's dog trotted up, tail wagging, to sniff his feet, and then went back to lie down in front of its master's house. Now Quantz's hands smelled like dog, mangy snout, and the filthy canine's dark haunches.

Quantz went to draw a bucket of water from the well and with the pail he headed toward the nook the old innkeeper had airily told him was his bathroom. He stripped all his clothes off and washed his face, then he rinsed himself from head to toe, using the water sparingly so he could lather up his hair, what remained of it, then rinse himself off by completely upending the bucket.

He was still sudsed up when he heard the bus honking on the other side of the inn, and, as he poured the last of the water over himself in a rush, scrabbling to pull on his clothes before he'd even dried off, the bus that had stopped so briefly started up again and sped away. The smoke spit out by the exhaust pipe, the powdery cloud, the roiling gravel, the bus's hazy, blunt silhouette, the variously colored, shapeless luggage strapped to the roof were all just barely visible. Then the whine of the motor dwindled in the distance.

Quantz didn't pull his clothes back off to dry. Heat was already rising up from the ground and would only intensify with the sunrise. His pants and the shirt sticking to his back cooled him off, all things considered. He hadn't been able to put his shoes back on and he was busy wiping his feet when the innkeeper walked up. They looked each other over, the innkeeper somewhat indifferently and idiotically, Quantz irritatedly, as the other man had told him the night before that the bus certainly wouldn't be coming before noon.

— The bus came, the innkeeper said after several seconds' silence.

— I know, I heard it, Quantz spat out. He was livid.

— Well, you missed it.

The innkeeper looked like a yak rancher or camel farmer, but on his face Quantz read neither the mysteriousness nor calm clearsightedness nor ancestral self-assurance so typical of the steppes; on his face there was only stubborn doltishness, fed perhaps by a bit of underhanded malice, a combination that was no longer all that rare in what remained of the human or humanoid population. From the outset, I've spoken of him as an innkeeper. This was how he identified himself to Quantz when, at nightfall, he had seen a group of huts that had given him some hope of finally escaping the desert. But the word innkeeper wouldn't be right for him, as these various rundown huts, the remnants of a former tiny hamlet, didn't deserve to be thought of as an inn. Evidently it would be better to call the innkeeper by his actual name. So I'll do so: the innkeeper was named Jabrayev.

— No point in waiting here, Jabrayev said, letting a glimmer of contempt shine through his gaze.

Quantz shrugged. He finished lacing up his shoes. He got back up. Down by the ground, the heat was far greater.

— And when's the next one? he asked.

— The next what?

— The next bus, when's it coming?

Jabrayev looked Quantz over a long while, his eyes riveted to Quantz's nose or forehead, not meeting Quantz's eyes. It was clear that he deemed his interlocutor incomprehensible and unsavory, and that he had to be rid of him as soon as possible.

— The next bus?

— Yes, said Quantz.

Two men facing one another. The sky was a golden blue at the horizon, in the direction the bus had vanished. The earth was exuding the nighttime heat, it was almost crackling under the onslaught of the day proper. Two men, or the equivalent. One, Quantz, furious, his sparse hair stuck to his forehead in gray clumps, his shirt open and stuck to his torso, rather tall and rather thin, awfully like a Cayacoe leading star filmed by the Cayacoes. The other, Jabrayev, awfully dumpy and soft, looking so dimwitted that Quantz was already wondering if his idiocy wasn't merely a put-on, even though having survived alone in such inhospitable terrain would imply a certain degree of intelligence.

— Eh, that I don't know, Jabrayev replied.

— You don't know, Quantz echoed.

His befuddlement was so clear that the other took pity on him and felt moved to round out his answer.

— A Thursday, in any case, he said. A Thursday at the same time, before noon in any case. But which one, I can't say. Just a Thursday, like today.

— Next week?

— Oh no, definitely not. Not next week.

— Well, when then?

Jabrayev raised his brow. It was the first time in a long while that

his face had made such a clear movement. It was a muscle movement that meant something. A step forward in his mental process.

— It's far off, he said. Thirty-three or thirty-four years. You'll
have to check the timetable.

— Wait, Quantz said. You mean the bus isn't coming by again for
another thirty-three years?

— Thirty-three or thirty-four years. Depends on what the timetable says. Check it.

Quantz examined the innkeeper's physiognomy. He still held out
hope of catching some speck of humor. Maybe this fellow would
burst out laughing, slap his shoulder, and tell him to loosen up a bit,
smile at this joke. But no. Nothing of the sort.

The sun was breaking away from the horizon. It was white, just
like the sky around it. Unusually sharp shadows had stretched out
past the surrounding hilltops, past the lonely bushes, past the clumps
of earth baked over the centuries into bricks. The innkeeper's dog
had stood back up and was resting one paw on a pile of wooden
planks. A stultifying heat was rising up, but the morning was a beautiful one. Seen at a remove, of course it was as beautiful as always.
But there was nobody to see this at a remove. Quantz and Jabrayev
weren't on a movie screen, in a Cayacoe film or otherwise. They
were far from any pitch-black theater, they were surrounded by reality, surrounded by scorching earth, both of them sweaty and alone.

— That's plenty of time to get back, Jabrayev mused.

— Guess so, Quantz replied.

Jabrayev turned around and walked away, whistling, then
waved at his dog, which got up and followed its master into one of
the shacks that was still standing. Apart from the half-ruined hut
Quantz had spent the night in, there were four of these shacks. The
dog's name was Kiddo. It was old and filthy, but its name was Kiddo.

Quantz rummaged through his bag, pulled out a sliver of pem-
mican that he crumbled up in his hand and chewed on for a good
half an hour, then he went to drink some water from the tap and

meander around the crumbling hamlet. Then he came back to Jabrayev, who was dozing in the shade of a wall and asked him where he could check that timetable he'd mentioned at sunup.

— It's in the next town over, Jabrayev said. Down the way the bus went. You'll have to walk there.

— All right, Quantz said. How far?

— Hmm . . .

Quantz did his best not to lose his patience. After all, if he got in a fight with the innkeeper or antagonized him, there wouldn't be anybody left to even try to trust, apart from Kiddo, with whom any conversation had to be relatively useless.

— How far in kilometers? he asked.

The other one shrugged helplessly.

— I don't know anything about kilometers. It's days. Twelve or thirteen days of walking. Fifteen if your shoes fall apart.

Stunned, Quantz started thinking about a tedious post-exotic novel he'd read some years earlier in prison, the story of a traveler who never reached his destination and spent his whole life wandering from one spot to another, going here in disguise, there in changing his sex, somewhere else in pulling on a prior's garments in a monastery, then marrying a witch, then becoming a highway bandit.

The novel, like so many works of this genre, had gone on and on, and Quantz had shut it without any curiosity about how it ended. But, at the beginning, there had been a man who had missed a train that only came at random intervals, and he'd had to make his way along the tracks to the next town over if he wanted to catch it, a journey that had taken him several weeks and during which he'd lost all sense of direction and all sanity.

— But if I were you, Jabrayev said, I wouldn't head off that way. If I were you, I'd wait for the next bus.

Quantz was the one to shrug helplessly now. He had no interest in dying of hunger and thirst on a deserted road, but, at the same time, he

FROM NINE AT NIGHT, the two convoys stayed cheek by jowl, and, as they were going at exactly the same speed, it felt like the train wasn't moving. This feeling lingered, hardly counteracted by the roar of the wheels and some regular clanking. The three fascinated children I was responsible for had huddled in front of a window. They were pressing their sweet little faces and the palms of their hands to the glass and they were serene. They were small, developmentally delayed Ybürs I had to take to a Party hospital, safe from blitzkriegs and pogroms. Their families had been killed before their eyes, and there was no question that had contributed to the chaos in their minds, but for now the crime they had witnessed had no effect on their behavior or their already deeply distorted view of the world. They were a charming little group that trusted me and listened to me, even when it was hard to make myself understood. They'd clung to me at once, when the Party nurse had turned her back on us after entrusting them to me. I felt pity for these three little beings whose only defense in the face of outside attacks was to withdraw into themselves to an unhealthy degree. Johann was eight; Muriel ten; Igor eleven. Here and there during the first two hours of the trip they held on to me and took my hand or touched me, but then, insofar as they were certain that I wouldn't upend their hermetic world, they gave my presence no further thought.

We had been traveling since midmorning and, when night fell, they all grew anxious until the carriage nightlights came on, even though I thought the light was insufficient and depressing. We were the only passengers in our car and, in all likelihood, the entire train. This prospect had unnerved me as we were sitting in the empty station and as I'd noticed, while we were waiting, that nobody came out to stand on the platform. I tried not to dwell on it any further once we were en route, but the thought kept nagging at me, and became more insistent when we were surrounded by darkness. I'd never believed in such things, but ever since this morning I'd felt scared that I was caught in a metaphysical trap.

The day had started off bleakly, flatly. We were going at an average speed without ever slowing down or speeding up. The children had perked up when the sandwiches were handed out, then they'd gone back to their listless introspection or those gestures they repeated endlessly. Igor rocked back and forth in sync with the wheels. Muriel went up and down the aisle slowly for hours, as if sleepwalking, banging into the partition doors and not trying to open them to get through. Little Johann, whose facial features evinced Down's Syndrome, sometimes huddled up by me, then went off and stiffened in some sort of doze. The landscapes we traversed barely changed. They alternated between plowed farmlands stretching to the horizon—dark, replete, yet devoid of any peasants or crows—and small towns or outskirts of large cities where it was impossible for us to catch any glimpse of a living soul, as the railroad tracks were separated by high walls as dark and replete as the farms, or by thick fences reinforced with sound barriers, heavy opaque panes of plastic that were filthy, covered with pogrom graffiti. We never stopped in the stations, and in fact I think our itinerary steered clear of them. As all these outside images disappeared, blurred into the night, I started to think that we might not be headed anywhere anymore, or rather that we were making our way into a black space the dimensions of which had to be as inconceivable as those that shaped, structured, delineated that journey after death. And so the appearance of a convoy beside us was staggering enough to distract me from my dark moods and thoughts.

Staggering enough, and dreadfully odd, too. Our two trains were twinned, separated only by the merest distance, barely a meter and a half. Just like the children, but without any slobbering on the glass on my part, I went and stared at the inside of the train alongside ours. Everything was dark there, and yet the few paltry nightlights gleaming along our aisle were reflected in the glass and indirectly lit up what was happening on the other side.

And what was happening was, in fact, nothing. On the seats, as still as mannequins, a few passengers could just be made out, maybe half a dozen. They didn't look our way, I couldn't tell whether they were ignoring us intentionally or not. They were dressed like peasants in their Sunday best, apart from a woman I couldn't see clearly at first, a woman whose clothes were reminiscent of a First-Soviet-Union schoolmarm. I focused on her, her face, I tried to discern her gaze, or at least her expression, and suddenly I was convinced I knew her. Clara Schiff. At that same instant came a lurch, and she shook her head very slowly. Then her eyes turned to mine. I was certain she was furtively addressing me, but shadows darkened her pretty face again.

Clara. I used to dream of lingering for hours in Clara's gaze, my only hope being to cling to her for a sliver of existence, despite the camps, despite the world's absurdities, despite the ethnic cleansings, despite the fears of the end, despite everything. But, fundamentally, we'd only met twice, in difficult circumstances, and we barely knew each other. In the middle of a crowd, the second time, in the middle of a conflagration, we'd clutched each other, both of us certain we would die, and I'd fallen in love with her. I learned that she worked in a phantom branch of the Party, those were the exact words, "phantom branch." I never saw her again, but I'd remained in love with her for eons.

The trains were frozen together, bound by some unclear enigma and by some need to maintain exactly the same speed. Two dark mirages slipping through the darkness, together, for several minutes now, for half an hour now, maybe more. My watch had stopped, I had no way of measuring time anymore.

I pulled myself away from the window and went back to the group of children. I don't know why, but tears were running down

Johann and Muriel's cheeks. They were all staring and, when I stroked their heads and shoulders, they didn't react. I pulled them close one by one. Johann held my hand tight for a few minutes, then let go. Muriel stopped crying. She started mumbling several vague and soon repetitive syllables in harmony with Igor; I couldn't make heads or tails of it. Neither of them were trying to match the other.

As I huddled with these children, I kept on probing the depths of the train that was so close, holding out hope of meeting Clara Schiff's eyes again. Praying for it. In the relative silence, in the trifling light, with Muriel's, with Igor's odd whisperings so close by, with Johann's tears and incomprehensible snuffling, I was overcome by irrational nostalgia. I swayed in rhythm with the train's jolts along the rails and I wanted to be on the other side, I wanted to find Clara Schiff, I wanted to take her in my arms and I wanted to savor the love I had for her, savor her presence, endlessly.

This situation, if it could be called one, dragged on. Then the squeal of brakes cut through the space and the two trains slowed down identically, with no discrepancy whatsoever, and, once all was still, what we could see on the other side was utterly unchanged in every way. The seated travelers didn't get up to see why they'd stopped. Clara Schiff wasn't moving either. I felt deep bitterness.

There were a few minutes of profound, mechanical silence. The children had pressed their hands and noses to the glass smeared with the drool and snot they hadn't bothered to wipe away, and they stayed put, rigid. Muriel was silent. Igor started banging his head placidly against the pane. I tried to pull him back, but he resisted. Muriel drew back into the aisle's shadows and started going this way and that again, as she'd done all afternoon. I made sure little Johann didn't still have tears flowing down his cheeks and I held him tight against my thigh, but he pulled away. Right then, I was convinced that Clara Schiff was giving me a sidelong glance from in the shadows, and I had the sensation that she was calling out to me.

I have to go see her, I thought. I have to get into the other con-voy. I have to go see Clara. Find Clara Schiff, my love.

I decided not to watch the children anymore, and went to the carriage door. I was beside myself. I absolutely had to open it, to take the two paces across the span separating the trains, and to make my way into the other train. The door, however, was locked. I shook it again and again to no avail, then I got a hold of myself and went back to the children, to the window facing the compartment where Clara Schiff was pretending to believe we didn't exist. On the other side, everything was inert. On our side, there were children bouncing around and there was myself unable to stay put.

I hadn't realized that we'd started off again. There wasn't any jolt and the other train accompanied us so perfectly that I hadn't regis-tered anything. Now we were traveling together again as uniformly as if we were soldered.

— It has to be possible to get to the other side, I said.

I suddenly felt the need to hear a human voice.

— What do you think, Igor? I said, almost unthinkingly.

The little boy suddenly acted completely unexpectedly. Without saying a word, as if he were a covert man of action who had merely been waiting for an opportune moment, he headed toward a seat and started dismantling it. It was hard and he wasn't entirely suc-cessful, but he kept at it determinedly, slowly, sticking his hand in the logical spots so that the base would come apart from its support and the back.

— But of course, I said encouragingly, and I hunched over the seat as well. But of course, yes, that'll help us cross the gap, we can break a window, then the window on the other side, and that'll help us cross the gap.

This was a fool's errand, but I

31. Schmumm

THE OOMPAHS AND ECHOES of the Internationale died down. Schmumm was out of the city center. He went past a store that smelled like cheese, turned the street corner, and found himself all alone. The sky was extremely black, as if charcoal had been rubbed over it, and the houses were extraordinarily dark, too, with façades the color of tar, walnut stain, carbon. The heat had only been increasing since the previous night.

From an inner courtyard a bird decked in rags practically fell on top of him, knocking him over, and, three meters later, stopped and glared at him with an asthmatic's guttural breath. It pulled tight the flaps of its beggar's overcoat and cawed:

— Were you at the protest?

— Of course, said Schmumm.

— Bullshit, the bird shot back. Everybody there ends up in the camps.

Schmumm shrugged. A good bit of his life had already been squandered in them; he knew from camps.

— They're needed, he said.

— What are? the bird cawed.

— Camps. They're needed.

The bird looked him over scornfully. It was as tall as Schmumm, but, thanks to the sternness of its glare, it managed to make Schmumm feel like a worthless dwarf, at the very bottom of the biological hierarchy. As such, Schmumm was now the one worriedly fiddling with his jacket buttons, as if straightening it after a heavy gust. He was wearing a filthy canvas shirt that he'd pulled on in order to walk with the reeducated, half-reeducated, rehabilitated, and proud-of-it section of the procession.

— You're just talking, the bird snapped after a few baleful seconds.

— I know what I'm talking about, Schmumm declared. I was there for twelve years.

— Twelve years! The bird let out a long whistle of astonishment.

— Indeed.

— Just as long as me, the bird said. Twelve years and two months.

Schmumm got flustered. He'd been exaggerating the length of his stay. Not wildly so, of course, but anyone paying attention to the numbers would have cried foul. He swallowed, cleared his throat, and, two seconds later, clarified:

— To be honest, for me, it was a bit less. Eleven years and four months.

The bird was singing a different tune now. It seemed to have shrugged off all ill will. Its eyes misted up, as if overcome with nostalgia. Its whistling breath wasn't aggressive anymore.

— I was at the Bakhromian work site, it said hoarsely.

— Me too, said Schmumm. We must have crossed paths.

— We might have, the bird said. Just one face among thousands.

— Thousands, or far more.

Night had fallen. The nearest streetlights hadn't turned on. Suddenly, as if to accentuate the worsening light, a hot gust filled the street, the neighborhood, battering the bird and Schmumm with a few distant notes of unidentifiable melodies, the aftermath of parties, and, again, the smell of cheese, spoiled milk, casein, yogurt that was beyond all hope.

Schmumm and the bird faced each other wordlessly for a minute. They didn't look each other in the eye, they hadn't mimed any connivance, but it would be reasonable to presume that they were silently sharing memories of the Bakhromian isolator and work site.

— Well, I have to say, they're not that bad, the bird grumbled, voicing an inner conversation and, for whatever reason, letting it spill out.

— What are you talking about? The work camps? Schmumm was stunned.

The bird jolted.

— Don't be silly, it said. I was talking about the creameries. For a bit, they were claiming that animals required compassion. But it was because they didn't have enough cows anymore for slaughter. It was wiser to use them as infinitely renewable resources. Milk, cream, cheese . . .

— Who cares, Schmumm cut in.

— I personally don't eat meat or dairy, the bird declared.

— So what do you eat then?

— Nothing.

They started talking about what they were eating and not eating, the dietary taboos the bird respected, the rotting food they'd had to force down at the Bakhromian work site, then it was full night and a searing heat had, along with the darkness, descended upon them.

Schmumm could feel the sweat dripping down his forehead, heavy, bitter drops that quickly ran down his nose and beneath his eyelids, filling his eyes and irritating them. The sweat blended with his tears. The bird, in turn, was trying to pull up the collar of its disgusting overcoat, as if what had come rolling down the street was in fact a snowy gust. Schmumm pretended not to notice the bird's bizarre behavior, but it picked up on his veiled disapproval and spoke up.

— I know, it said. It messed me up. When I got out, I'd lost all my bearings. My body, too. My body reacts the opposite way to the temperature all around.

— It'll go back to normal, Schmumm ventured.

— You're just saying that.

— No, I mean it. Someday it'll switch back to normal, Schmumm said reassuringly. He didn't really believe his words; he just knew he had to say something.

— Oh, Schmumm, don't bother. They messed me up and it's permanent.

New drops of sweat beaded across Schmumm's face, on his lower back, in his armpits, all over his arms. In the darkness, he could barely make out the bird's wizened yet almost hulking outline. They hadn't introduced themselves to each other at any point.

— Wait, you know my name, Schmumm said. How did you know that?

The bird shook obscurely, as if to rid itself of a nightmare. It panted for three seconds and then said, plaintively:

— Who cares about names.

— I care about mine, Schmumm said. How do you know it? Are you in the Forces?

As the bird wasn't making any sound, Schmumm took a step forward, stuck his hand out toward its belly, and then grabbed it violently. It could feel a button resisting his attempt and he pulled harder. Then the bird twisted and caught his wrist. It moved in a way that underscored its expertise in hand-to-hand combat and the likelihood, if Schmumm didn't let go right away, that it would snap whatever it could—his fingers, an arm joint, pairing that with a forearm smash below the chin and a well-aimed kick or knee to his solar plexus. Schmumm quickly gave up the fight. He'd gone to the mat many times over his life, but he'd rarely had the upper hand over his adversaries. Knowing that defeat was imminent took the wind out of his sails. He pulled his hand away and stepped back.

— Are you in the Forces? he repeated. He was gasping.

The bird shrugged and smoothed out the rags ruffled by the confrontation. It dusted itself off, as if Schmumm had only thrown a fistful of dirt at it.

— You're still watching me, Schmumm declared.

They stood there pensively. The bird was done cleaning itself off and it was breathing loudly. Both could be heard panting. Two silhouettes frozen in the dark air and dark heat, both of them now seemingly settling, unhurriedly, between aggressiveness and despair.

— But I've been part of a group of rehabilitated people proud of it, Schmumm suddenly recalled. I was part of your protests. I applied to join a circle of sympathizers. Why are you still watching me?

The bird sighed.

— Just a precautionary measure, it said.

— I have nothing to be ashamed of, Schmumm whined.

— Oh, really? What about this, then? the bird said.

A new blast of hot air rushed through. Schmumm felt like he was liquefying, his temples were pounding. The bird had pulled a notebook out from its rags and tatters.

They headed off toward the one streetlamp in the universe that still seemed to work, by an intersection four hundred meters away. The bird wanted to show Schmumm something and Schmumm wanted to see what it was. His anxiety only grew. What if the Forces had in fact discovered some aspect of his life that would keep him from joining the circle of sympathizers? What if, in this black notebook that the bird was holding, there was some proof of his double dealing? Would this be the fatal mistake that sent him back to the camps?

What if he tried to yank the notebook out of the bird's hands, what if he strangled it? He was well-positioned right behind it, what if he strangled it?

He started unbuckling his belt. He'd have no luck with his hands, but with a belt, he might come out on top. And he could finish it off by hanging it from an unlit streetlamp.

After a hundred paces, the bird stopped.

— Don't even try it, Schmumm, it said. We both know you're already deep in the shit. Don't saddle your conscience with one more death.

— It'd do me some good to have strangled someone from the Forces before being sent back that way, Schmumm retorted.

— Don't be so sure of that, the bird said. I'd be amazed if it did you any good. And who knows, down the line, you might end up in the Forces yourself.

Schmumm found himself stammering.

— I don't

32. Sarah Agamemnian

IT WASN'T THE FIRST TIME that she'd been given a bird's shape and body or that she'd found herself wreathed in flames. Her name was Sarah Agamemnian and she had been part of the Action Forces from her early childhood.

As she had just stirred and she wasn't thinking clearly yet, she basked in the flames for a while, reciting the prayers she had been taught to overcome onslaughts of dazzling light and heat. "McDouglas," she thought after that. "Just have to find McDouglas, make him talk, kill him, and come back to headquarters."

The coke-fed fire was fanned higher and higher by the gusts of burning air hissing out, as far as she could tell, from two sets of seven outlets on each side of the blast furnace. "Seven," she thought. "Always that golden number, that magical number. Again and again. Or maybe an eighth one just isn't working. Maybe there's no magic here. A broken eighth outlet, that's it."

She stretched out and then shook her body. Under her legs simmered a sticky mixture of molten metal and charred residue in ever-changing, iridescent colors: crimson, yellow, black. The strewing was a thick one. If she had wanted to dig in, she wouldn't have reached bottom. The flames weren't really blinding, but they were awfully dense and they felt to Sarah Agamemnian more like heavy wall-hangings than violent whirlwinds. It was almost impossible to bear the heat, and the air currents were whistling, screaming to a deafening degree. "All right," she thought, "no need to dawdle in this pretty little blaze."

She recited a prayer once again then righted herself, spreading her wings then pulling them back in. Her head wasn't as cottony as when she'd first opened her eyes and she now remembered what exactly she'd come to do here, as well as the information she needed to lay hands on good old McDouglas. Five meters away from where she stood was a door to a room that had to be well lit but seemed, by comparison, totally dark. She walked toward that black rectangle, stepped over the stream of molten steel flowing down a channel made out of some resistant material, and exited.

It was night, but the immense space was bathed by beacons and floodlights illuminating various industrial plants, multilevel black-steel structures studded labyrinthinely with hatches and girded by even blacker piping. Farther off, some three hundred meters away, rose up a second blast furnace. It was hot, the ground was greasy, the air stank of sulfur, charcoal dust, burned oil, and fire. "It was better in there," Sarah Agamemnian mused, and then immediately had to parry a blow to her stomach, the whistling onrush of a long iron pole. A worker was trying to get her with an industrial poker. She sprang up two meters at the very last moment, avoiding the improvised weapon, and twirled, swooping down on her adversary. It had all happened so quickly that he hadn't realized what was happening, or at least hadn't had the time to even imagine fighting off this monstrous bird straight out of the furnace. Even his reflexes didn't have the time to react. The iron pole flew out of his hands and the man who had just let go of it felt, on his ribcage, the force of a downy caress that instantaneously turned into a violent blow. Then he didn't feel anything else, at least in the realm of the living. "So it begins," Sarah Agamemnian said to herself as she settled on some grill plates with small perforations around their concrete covering. The little holes were shaped like four-leaf clovers. "Cute," she found herself thinking. Then she disarmed a second man headed for her with another poker. Like the first one, he was in a grubby fire-resistant suit and had a badge that showed her what he was: the service engineer Michael Briggs. "That's not who I'm looking for," Sarah Agamemnian thought as she wrenched away his weapon and killed him.

As she hadn't come here to exterminate steelworks minions, she hurried out of the factory, paying no further heed to provocations and attacks. She could see them kilometers off and she simply went around a machine and moved in its shadow, or vanished down some passageway and took one path or another where the encounter would be impossible. At one point more than a dozen people were yelling out to each other to block her off and neutralize her. The security team was jabbering through walkie-talkies but couldn't pin her down. It was obvious that the men braying orders at one another knew they were dealing with an adversary far too powerful for them and, for all the hullabaloo they made whenever one of their bosses' cameras swept over them, that was it: they waved their arms but didn't dare get close.

A few minutes later, she'd bypassed the wire fencing and left behind the screams and yells and alarms that stood out against the machines' apocalyptic hammering and wheezing. She crossed a lawn, some parking lots, reached an empty boulevard, and then started down the side of a road she figured led to a town, as there were streetlights on each side in both directions. Beyond the gleaming cones of yellow on the grass and asphalt, the night was inky black. The sky harbored no stars. Every so often, a car or truck roared past, its engine racing, its tires whistling through the water pooled on the road, before it swiftly dissolved into the shadows. She could hear the shrill trichord of police sirens far off. If a strike force was headed to the steelworks, they were taking a different route than the one Sarah Agamemnian was now on, and they would only arrive there long after the battle.

Rain was falling, first as an insistent drizzle, then, not long after, as an increasingly brutal downpour. "It'll be refreshing," Sarah Agamemnian thought, urging herself to think optimistically, but she wasn't all that keen. The down of her face and her wings, which could handle contact with fire and high-heat winds unharmed, weren't nearly so well suited to water as they grew wet and heavy all too easily, sending rather unpleasant messages of weariness and shivering to her skin. "It'll be cleansing," she decided. She tried to practice self-suggestion so she would enjoy the rain. "After this stint in the furnace, I'm covered in soot, I might even have blotches of tar on my feet and head."

She had just entered something that, up north, could have been called a burg. A sign posted in front of the outermost dwellings gave this place a name: Black Village. It was dark, swept by sheets of icy raindrops, and past the dark walls and windows it was hard to imagine the sleepers—there was such a feeling of desolation and solitude that only a paltry number of exhausted old men and women or dead people with no known next of kin was imaginable. A row of one-story homes to the left, an identical row to the right, a few neon signs over the empty parking lots. A gas station with all its lights off. A grocer's with its metal grille pulled down in front of the display, which still had three woebegone spotlights turned on. A motel with blue and white cursive letters that sometimes flashed off and on, informing any stragglers that they were welcome at all hours of day and night, and that it went by the charming name of Black Village New Motel.

"Black Village New Motel," Sarah Agamemnian thought. "I'll put up my feet there until sunrise."

She walked around the buildings, confirmed that the check-in desk was deserted and all the keys were hanging on the board, forced the door open, and plucked out a key at random, throwing the others in a drawer so it wouldn't be obvious to anyone hot on her heels which room number was hers, then she went back out into the deluge, locked the door behind her as she'd been taught so as not to leave any trace, went down the nearest breezeway, and eventually came to number 35, the number she hadn't chosen entirely at random. She liked odd numbers and multiples of seven.

The room smelled like dirty carpet, salesmen's shoes, and bleach-based cleaning liquids. She locked the door and slid the safety chain in place, checked over the room without turning on the lights, made sure there was a shower and toilet that weren't dirty, and, once she was certain of that, she shook off and sprayed in every direction the water that her feathers had accumulated. "It could have been worse," she thought. "I'll wait here until the rain stops, and at sunrise I'll head into town. I'll pick up a gun and I'll head into town. Then I'll take care of McDouglas."

She went into the bathroom and rummaged through the chipboard furnishings. She pulled out two terry-cloth towels, a small bar of soap, but no gun. "As if there was any hope of unearthing a pistol here! Why even dream, my darling."

She froze in front of the mirror. The darkness notwithstanding, she could see herself: an elegant clump of white feathers, very few soot stains, a thin face covered by down that was already fluffed up again, on her left collarbone, where it met her wing, a slightly scorched area. "Why even dream, my darling," she repeated.

Then she sat down to wait for sunrise. She went over to the bay window, pulled apart the curtains, and leaned against the brick wall. She didn't move. Outside, everything was dark, with a motorcycle garage about twenty meters off as well as a streetlight that barely shone at all in the increasingly heavy rain. The water whipped the courtyard with a roar, and when the gusts of wind intensified, it battered the glass. Two hours went by thus. Apart from the volleys of rain, there was no movement in the night. Sarah Agamemnian, who knew she wouldn't need any sleep before the end of her mission, calmly monitored the view. She didn't doze off, she stayed alert and thought about her target, this McDouglas the Action Forces had assigned to her and who had far more tricks up his sleeve than any normal human being.

As she was going over the obstacles she'd have to overcome before reaching and neutralizing McDouglas, she saw a figure appear in the courtyard. It was a biker in head-to-toe leather. He was dripping, the light the streetlamp exuded tingeing him a bit silver, and he'd seen her through the window. She didn't hide behind the curtain. He made his way to her room, raising his arms as if to wave at her. "What if this guy's the first trap that McDouglas's set for me?" she thought.

She waited until the biker was a meter away from the glass to

33. Yaabadgul Something

THE WOMAN WAS ALMOST COMPLETELY BLIND. Her splendid eyes, an intense emerald green, were only of help in distinguishing the sun from the moon, or in picking out the biggest obstacles that stood in her way as she walked through the countryside: walls, for example, or trees, or buffalo. For everything else, she relied on her hearing, as well as Mooglee, an astute creature that she kept on her belt at all times and that lived symbiotically with her, guiding her through the winding corridors of adversity. Mooglee described things around her constantly, by telepathy or actual speech, and most often with a combination of the two. With this support at all moments, the woman went at a steady gait down the pavement, a massive avenue leading to the hospital. She had heard that a committee was interviewing applicants to go into the hereafter, gather as much intelligence as possible, and return, and she felt wholly prepared to carry out this sort of mission.

Her name was Saraya Abadgul. She was young, at most thirty-five, but she'd lived in extreme conditions and in critical locations, with nomads, beggars, refugees, and death-row inmates, for so long that her physical attributes were those of a crone. She looked like a particularly robust eightysomething, her face lined and darkened by decades of misfortune. The prospect of charming men had never had much hold on her—sexuality had, on the contrary, terrified her from her teen years onward—so she was quite happy with, unbothered by, her physical decay. Looking like an old worthless wretch who was vaguely feminine didn't upset her in the least. If anything, it protected her from being raped at every opportunity by her comrades in misfortune or in the barracks.

— Watch out at the next step, Mooglee warned her.

But the warning had come too late and Saraya Abadgul sank to her knees in a dried-out pothole. The mud had formed a crust that blended cruelly into the normal soil and just below it was a dust pit as big as a sink. This sort of trap was typical and even characteristic of this region. The air was always wafting floury sand, small specks that piled up in the pavement's craters. Before dawn, the humidity borne from the sea precipitated on the surfaces of these traps, then, once it was gone, dreadful heat having taken its place, the earth hardened a few millimeters more. And then nothing remained to warn oncomers of this hazard.

The first thing Saraya Abadgul felt was the feeling that the dry dust provoked as it slipped into her shoes. She hadn't sprained her ankle, but didn't struggle to get out of the hole just yet; her fears turned to a little group of kids closing in on her. The oldest of them had to be eleven or twelve, and they formed a half-circle as they burst out laughing. Going by Mooglee's whispers, they were filthy, tattered, and slapping their sides like chimpanzees, sending up yellow dust clouds around themselves. Saraya Abadgul listened carefully and made out seven children: four boys, three girls.

— There's an eighth one, on the right, Mooglee cut in. He's crouching down. He's a sneaky, quiet one, he's not laughing with the others. He's crouching down to pick up a stone.

Still buried in the sand, Saraya Abadgul made a reel out of her rosewood pole, which was as hard as metal, and the seven brats pulled back, trading their sniggering for whines. The eighth one, the one who had crouched down and was now holding a stone, got up, took his time, and launched his projectile.

— It's headed for your right cheek, Mooglee warned her.

Saraya Abadgul leaned left and immediately felt, right by her head, the air that the stone had displaced, accompanied by a stench of burnt earth and street mites. What a bastard that snotty little kid is, she thought. He needs to be taught a good lesson.

With a single thrust of her calves and lower back, she extricated herself from the dusthole. The children looked at her, unsure what to think. A gawky group of cruel kids, willing to do anything to survive and keep others from doing so. They were stunned by this ragtag woman's agility; they didn't feel bad for having mocked her, but they did take a step back to stay out of reach of her stick, and they scowled. The most dangerous one, the one who had thrown the stone, suddenly realized that he'd attacked someone as inoffensive as a ragamuffin grandmother.

— Hey, he called out. You see that thingummy on her belly?

Saraya Abadgul could tell what he was thinking through the terrified snippets Mooglee was sending her. A living clump, the filthy boy was thinking, some kind of massive wigged spider, hairy, devoid of eyes, but still clearly staring at us. I should have hit it, he was thinking.

The stone he had thrown completed its aerial trajectory, bounced on the cement by the gutter, and rolled to a peasant's stall as he sat, perched on his haunches, awaiting buyers by a dirty cloth laid out with five sweet peppers and a few nuts. Saraya Abadgul walked up to her aggressor and, holding her baton flat, struck the boy hard on his temple and then his ear. The boy was sent flying three meters off, reeling and stumbling and trying to stop the pain by pressing his hands to the impact sites, then he lost his balance and fell down on the curbside among a few dust heaps.

The other children were already distancing themselves from him and running off, not even looking back, as if a shadowy force, or dogs, were nipping at their heels. The boy was all alone and he lay in the gutter, stunned.

— If you want to finish him off, Mooglee said, now is the time.

— I don't want to finish him off, Saraya Abadgul said. I want to get to the hospital before they stop admission.

She started down the avenue, on alert. The children had disappeared. Under the trees could be seen peasant women and sellers hawking their wares. They were all hunched down by their paltry goods, here two cookies, there a carafe of water and a dirty glass, farther off a tomato and four overripe bananas. Mooglee described all this to Saraya Abadgul. She didn't stop for water, even though the sun was pounding and she could use something to drink. On one hand, she'd acclimatized her body over the years to resisting thirst, and on the other, she figured she'd be able to find a tap at the hospital and slake her thirst. As she walked past yet another water-seller, she heard the filthy boy coming up behind her, and, instinctively, she spun around and brandished her stick.

— Wait, he's got a knife, Mooglee said. He's charging at you, and he's clearly going to speed up, come at you on the left, and tear you to pieces.

Saraya Abadgul focused, waited a few fractions of a second, then, as she pulled back half a meter, brought down her rosewood weapon. She could feel the boy's skull shatter. She raised her stick again and, unperturbed by the victim's moaning, landed a second powerful blow on him between his jaw and collarbone. The attacker staggered off. He'd dropped his knife and was immobile.

— You finished him off there, Mooglee confirmed.

— Who knows. He's a bad egg, one second he's on the ground and the next he's up and at it again.

She went through the hospital gates and headed down the paved courtyard. After ten meters, a watchman came up to her and, after being told the reason for her visit, took sympathy on her and steered her away from appearing before the committee. There were too many applicants, more than a hundred all crammed together on the steps and packing the hallways for three days now, it wasn't likely she'd be summoned to the jury, and if her file wasn't bulletproof, she'd likely end up in the cesspit rather than on the list. As he finished talking and even raised his hand to give her shoulder a sympathetic slap, he suddenly noticed Mooglee, froze, and went quiet. Saraya Abadgul thanked him for his advice and headed toward the building he'd already pointed her toward.

A second watchman stopped her, asked her whether she had a file in good order, but didn't press the matter when she confirmed that the committee would see her even without a file.

— What's your name? the watchman asked, so as to justify her presence or function at the bottom of the steps.

— Yaabadgul something, she said, as she sidestepped the man adroitly.

He was about to protest, but then he sensed Mooglee's presence and swallowed.

— Go on, he said weakly.

Once she was in the hallway, Saraya Abadgul pushed her way through with her elbows and walking stick, and shouted that she was a priority applicant owing to her age and her handicap. As if there was no question of her rightful place, she stepped over those asleep, those half dead, and those curled up. Mooglee chattered constantly, helping her forward, which set off angry protests, fury, and spit from the crowd. Several applicants had tried to kick her, but the response was so swift, the noise of the stick across their faces so sharp, the message so clear, that soon nobody tried to give her any trouble physically. On the other hand, the poor light notwithstanding, several candidates had seen the black stain on her

171

belly, and had heard or sensed the brief whispers emanating from it, and terror spread like wildfire across all those present. For years, a rumor had swirled that a blind witch would make her way across the region and fell all those who resisted her with her magic staff. With her magic staff and with what, in the telling, was sometimes a dog's head on her belt, sometimes a giant spider grafted onto her breasts, sometimes a handful of extra eyes gleaming horrifically under her dress. As soon as the applicants connected her to that legend, they let her pass. But, just as she was a few meters from the door the committee lay behind, it opened and the big guy appeared in the frame, his legs bare beneath his sweat-stained

34. Black 3

I WAS CONVINCED TASSILI WAS LAID UP for good, but, as if a sudden burst of adrenaline or what served for it here had buoyed him, he righted himself to the point of being on all fours again, then he kept on pulling himself up by clawing at the wood logs at the base of which we were all prostrate. The endeavor took some time, but, at the end of it, he was flat against the roughly hewn trunks, some of which still had the beginnings of branches, apparent burls. Tassili had clearly clutched them to steady his grip and not fall back. I, too, wanted to get myself vertical and I started shifting a bit, on my own. I felt Goodmann's body against mine. Goodmann wasn't moving. He was curled up and still. All his energy was invested in sustaining the very small flame burning on his right hand and, very modestly, illuminating us. A deep silence reigned around us, but we could hear Tassili breathing convulsively, if that verb held any particular meaning in our situation. He panted in that way for an hour or two, the time it took me to also get myself upright and lean on the logs, then he mumbled some words about the smells wafting up by his face. I had trouble understanding him. I think he was talking about dampness, moisture, forests. Then he was silent. I had the impression that he had pressed his lips and his whole face to the wood wall and that he was looking at something just beyond.

— See something? I asked.

— Hey, Tassili, do you see what's on the other side? Goodmann asked.

Tassili pulled away from the wood and, very slowly, then with increased speed, fell back. After a moment, he was lying on the packed-dirt ground, out of breath and possibly bruised, but, as he wasn't groaning, he seemed to have chosen to stretch out this way on his back to rest or doze or start telling a new story devoid of an ending.

Goodmann shook his hand at him. The gesture caused some sputtering and fresh light. Tassili's figure appeared, an unreadable mask that seemed imbued by a sooty paste that had erased all detail.

— Did you see what's on the other side? Goodmann asked again.

— Yes, Tassili lied, to keep up the conversation.

— Is it Black Village? I ventured, on the off chance, without imagining what that was, and that too, no doubt, was out of a sheer need not to let our discussion die out.

— Uh, yes, Tassili lied.

Despite our efforts, silence settled among us. It was not at all hostile, it did not correspond to any illness. We had, from the outset, or just about, felt brotherly affection and solidarity, but we were overcome by an immense exhaustion, and we spent most of our time feigning mental and physical activity, pretending to talk, pretending to tell stories, or pretending to be quiet. For however many hours or days, I don't know, nothing happened. Goodmann's hand blazed more or blazed less, but it didn't go out. It wasn't all that lightsome and we could stare at it a long while without any harm to our retinas, assuming we were still endowed with equivalent tissue in the depths of our sockets.

Then Goodmann stirred and jiggled his hand. Barely perceptible petals of fire elongated in the darkness bathing us and froze in front of our heads, so weak that no shadows played out over our physiognomies. From his wrist to the first finger joints, Goodmann's flesh was being eaten up interminably, and had been for days or years or even more because, ever since our first steps in this black space, duration had obeyed no known rules, had been swirling inconsistently around us, hadn't stopped breaking off, stopping, then resuming without our ever being able to measure it, even when we attempted to quantify that duration with words, with accounts or narracts or equivalent minor verbal outpourings.

— What did it look like? Goodmann asked.

— Honestly, nothing's visible, Tassili sighed. Black Village or whatever else, nothing's visible. Nothing stands out in the darkness. If something exists or is moving out there, we have no way of knowing.

— We're better off here, I said.

— What's the point of you talking, Tassili, Goodmann said. All you say is shit.

— We've already talked about that Black Village, Tassili shot back.

— What's the point of talking, Goodmann said.

Exhaustion got the better of me. I couldn't stand anymore. My legs had started trembling and were giving way. I let myself fall down by Goodmann and, as I did so, I brushed his shoulder, which knocked him off balance. He had been crouching until then, and now he had collapsed beside me.

Once again, all three of us were plopped down right by one another.

We stayed in the same positions, lengthily slowly silent, for lengthy slow hours. I focused on the almost-lightless reddening embers on Goodmann's hand. My thoughts went round and round and came to nothing. I would have liked to recall something, for example, a portion of my preceding existence, or at least one of the mutilated accounts we had tried to give voice to, during our march, let's say recently, assuming that the idea of a recent event still has meaning. Nothing was forthcoming.

Tassili spoke suddenly.

— Will your hand ever stop burning?

He sounded worried.

Goodmann brought his hand to his eyes, or at least to his face, or at least to what stood in for it. He examined the small flame for a moment. Then he set his hand down on his knee.

— There's still some fuel, he said.

— Good, Tassili said.

— It's not close to gone, Goodmann added.

I believe he was trying to reassure us. The idea of continuing the march in this darkness, in total, tarry darkness, flickered across all three of our minds.

In any case, for me, that idea had flickered in my mind.

— I wouldn't want this to end in darkness, I said, I mean in total, tarry darkness.

— There's no other darkness, Tassili asserted.

— What's the point of you two talking, Goodmann said.

35. Black 4

ONCE AGAIN I GOT UP ON TIPTOES to look through the arrow slit. The opening smelled like sodden fir and mushrooms. There was nothing perceptible on the other side. The total darkness was so thick that it slipped beneath my eyelids with a sucking sound, like trying to pull a foot out of a puddle of tar.

— See something? Goodmann asked.

He broke a silence that had lasted between the three of us for I don't know how long. We weren't on bad terms and, on the contrary, we truly felt brotherly and close to one another, but we had suffered deterioration and we were saving the last of our strength to pretend to breathe, to hold steady, or to live. Goodmann's hand had had difficulty staying afire but it went on burning and brought us the comfort of a bit of light, at least when we activated our sense of sight, which we did increasingly rarely. Goodmann jiggled his hand and wispy sparks flared, soon becoming barely luminous, golden-brown flakes that settled without guttering, beside his face, although without revealing anything of his physiognomy all the whole. From his wrist to his fingers' first joints, Goodmann's flesh was being eaten up interminably, and had been for hours or days or even more because around us time was no longer measurable, no longer flowed, broke up or hiccupped irrationally. The fire was just as Goodmann had called it in lighting it: a slow, very slow fire, a fire of extreme slowness.

— Nothing's visible, I said. The darkness is total, so thick that it slips beneath my eyelids with a sucking sound.

— A sucking sound? Myriam said.

She was slumped close by, unseen, beyond the ken of the pathetic glints escaping Goodmann's hand. Ever since her last turn talking, she hadn't moved. As always, the story had come to a stop without ending, the very idea of continuing it had dissolved in the void along with the rest.

Myriam's question encouraged me to recall the account that she had started up the other day and which, immediately after its being interrupted in media res, had accompanied the wreckage of all duration and had sunk somewhere apart from our memories, in any case somewhere apart from mine. And now, suddenly, bits came back, shoddily connected to one another but made of lines that stirred up images within me. It all came rushing out of a hole both outside myself and inside, a black hole of our memories and our shadows—of mine in any case. It was the story of a blind woman who moved around and fought unhesitatingly by the instructions being constantly dictated by a sort of spider on or in her stomach. This woman wanted to appear before a committee in order to be chosen to die, to visit the dark space after expiring and come back to give a report. It was a narract that promised to be enthralling, but, like the others, it had been cut off before its end, and here I'm speaking of a cut as definitive and violent as a power cut, as if no duration, no whiff or stretch of time, no matter how infinitesimal, could have quickened the spiel anew, or as if an overnarrator or a demon of the abyss had tinkered with a fatal circuit breaker and had no interest in flipping it back to its original configuration.

I let a moment go by, a matter of recalling the matter, then I answered Myriam.

— Yes, a sucking sound. You know, like trying to pull a foot out of a puddle of tar.

— What's the point of you talking, Goodmann sighed. All you say is shit.

I went back to leaning my face, or what stood in for it, against the arrow slit. This contact with the shadows outside, painful owing to this sucking, disjointing sensation caused by the void, was modulated by the smells of wet wood and mushrooms. On the other side, there was nothing, in any case hardly more than what surrounded us where we were. All the same, these smells stirred up some memories I had of a preceding existence, where I found myself moving around in the taiga's darkness, sometimes under the surveillance of wardens, sometimes with the impression of being alone and being free, or, at least, alive.

Myriam got up and came over to me. I heard her walking waveringly, then she touched my back. She breathed, struggling, with stretches of not breathing that piled up, half-hour on half-hour. I let her approach me and forced myself to match the rhythm of her lungs, or what, for her and me, stood in for those. I had a great deal of trouble getting anything going, and after an hour or two, I gave up pretending to gorge on air and I held her close. We stayed silent a long while. Goodmann, too, had come up to us. He took care not to inconvenience us with the embers of his hand.

— Where are we? Myriam finally said.

— Not very far, I said as I glanced past my shoulder toward the blackness.

Goodmann didn't seem to be satisfied by the turn the dialogue had taken, by its contents or lack of contents.

— Speak for yourself, he retorted.

We stayed, not opening our mouths, for an hour or two, or maybe more. Every so often, one of us turned our head to the outside or toward Goodmann's hand, or toward still darker points.

Finally, we started whispering.

— Not very far from what? Myriam whispered.

— I don't know, I whispered back.

LUTZ BASSMANN is one of French author Antoine Volodine's numerous heteronyms belonging to a community of imaginary authors that includes Manuela Draeger and Elli Kronauer. Since 2008, Bassmann has authored five books, including *We Monks & Soldiers* (University of Nebraska). This is his second book to be translated into English.

JEFFREY ZUCKERMAN is a translator of French, including books by the artists Jean-Michel Basquiat and the Dardenne brothers, the queer writers Jean Genet and Hervé Guibert, and the Mauritian novelists Ananda Devi, Shenaz Patel, and Carl de Souza. A graduate of Yale University, he has been a finalist for the TA First Translation Prize and the French-American Foundation Translation Prize, and has been awarded a PEN/Heim translation grant and the French Voices Grand Prize. In 2020 he was named a Chevalier in the Ordre des Arts et des Lettres by the French government.